First Sighting and Waiting Period

After chasing the lone ship for a short while, the Rnites decided they weren't worth their time to worry about and left them to their fate and left them out in space to die, thus ending the war for all time, and headed back toward their own little bit of space.

What the Rnites didn't count on, however, was the resourcefulness of this one little ship and its crew.

The lone survivors, twenty years after escaping the Rnites, are living on an inhabited planet in a quadrant not far from their home planets and in much similar surroundings. They have bonded with its citizens and have even become members of some families.

The life forms on this new planet are members of a peaceful populace and war is far from anyone's mind. Those of the newer generations haven't even known war, on their planet or out into space, and the only exposures they have had to either would be the stories the elders tell around their homes on special occasions.

The crew from the lost ship have been welcomed into the society and made to feel like they belonged. Their stories have been told and awed at, along with all of the other war stories, and they eventually became just that – stories.

Life was good for all of them and they put their past lives behind them, until that morning when a small boy went running into his house and called out for his omn.

"Omn, there is a meeting this high sun time! What's a meeting? What happens at one? Do you get to eat at this meeting?"

"Shush, child! So many questions and so fast! I don't know what you are talking about. What meeting? Where?"

"At the Ruling Council's chambers. My friend told me his dad told him the last time they called a meeting was before his soumnn was born. Is that true? His soumnn is really old and..."

"Child! Stop and take a breath! I do not doubt you, but there must be a reason for this meeting after all this time."

The omn didn't want to frighten the child, but she remembered the stories that the elders used to tell about the last time the meeting was called. They had gone to war with another planet far away from

1

theirs and each side had had weapons too horrible to think about. She had been told her own soumnn had fought in this war and was never seen again. The story went that one of the other planet's weapons had just vapourized him somehow and when word of this reached home, the Ruling Council had devised a weapon much stronger and deadlier that the other and it was told that even the ships of the enemies disappeared after having this weapon used upon them.

She looked down upon her child and worried that the meeting was real and they were about to go to war again. She cried a soft tear to think that her son would know what it would be like to take another being's life and throw it away.

She had been taught, as she was teaching him, that war was such a bad thing and to waste another being's life was unforgivable in the eyes of the Creator. She sent up a quiet prayer that if there was to be a meeting, it was for good news and not bad.

As she reached for the voicing machine, she placed her hand on her child's head and rubbed his head spines. He loved it when she did that. She would have to ask her umnn's tae's child to forgo the meeting, if there was one, to watch the child.

"Margos answering." He never changed, she thought to herself. Years after everyone else had adopted the new voice answering command, he was still stuck in the old ways. She loved him for that.

"Hello, Margos. It is your betrothed voicing."

"Good sun to you, Anor. How are you and the little one?"

They had just seen each other a short while ago but he didn't fail to ask after them as if he hadn't seen them for several periods of time. He truly was a loving mate and umnn.

"We are well, thank you. And you?"

He hesitated just long enough to worry her.

"I am also well, thank you. I believe I know why you have voiced me during my working time. You have heard about the meeting after the mid point nutritional time."

"Yes. The child brought home the news from his playtime. Have you any knowledge as to what the Ruling Council wishes to discuss with us? It must be very important for them to call a meeting during our rest period." Her mate's position in the Ruling Council offices would most likely allow him some knowledge, she thought. She held her breath that it would be delightful news and not sad.

Her mate hesitated once again, but this time for a longer period. When he responded, it was with a cheerless tone to his voice, one she had never heard him utter in all of the years she had known him.

"The scanners we have pointed out into space have sent back reports that ships are approaching us once again. The Ruling Council wants to make everyone aware of this and to make sure we are prepared for our guests' arrival."

Something in his tone told her there was more but she knew better than to ask. If the citizens were to know more, they would be told at the meeting later. She had already asked too much. Besides, the last ship had brought friends, hadn't it?

She tried to sound as positive as she could. "It has been some time since we received visitors from other planets" she said. "This will definitely give us something new to talk about in the coming time before their arrival."

"Indeed."

The Ruling Council's chamber was full and those who were not allowed a seat stood out in the hallways and stairwells, listening to the news of the Ruling Council through exterior voice and image machines found throughout the building and mounted to the exterior next to all entries. Each machine had a small crowd around it in and out of the building. There had never been so many individuals together in one place at one time in living memory. There must not have been any one left at home except for the children and their caretakers. Rumours and concern were whispered throughout the crowd as they awaited the news.

The Ruling Council's Leader cleared his throat and all fell silent. No one wanted to miss a single word.

"Thank you for coming. I will make this short. Our scanners into space have reported a ship headed our way. This ship should be arriving within the next two or three evening rest periods.

"At this time, we do not know if this ship carries men of honour or not. We have no way of knowing this until their arrival, as they are not answering our hails.

"We, the Ruling Council, want you to be prepared not for men of honour but men of discourse. If they are men of honour, we will greet them like the honoured guest they will be.

"If, on the other hand, they are not, we shall be prepared to defend our way of life.

"Please return to your homes and make the arrangements.

"Men of twenty summers and more will meet here after the evening nutritional time for a planning council.

"That is all."

The crowd dispersed quickly and went about the business of preparing for whatever the visitors would bring. There was not a voice among those closest to Anor to have a negative thought about the visitors. That was just the way of her nation.

Her return journey to her home led her through the tranquil area where she had played as a child. Her children, as children before her, enjoyed standing on the small bridge and tried to imagine the small fish that once swam below the surface of the stream that was no longer there.

She stayed on the bridge and imagined the ripples on the surface as the few remaining mutated fish that had managed to learn to live in the polluted water by developing exterior lungs with which to breath the air bobbed their heads out of the ink coloured liquid, looking for the crumbs of bread that citizens would toss down to them. How they could have survived for so long in such pollution astounded her as the air was almost as polluted as the water. She shook these thoughts from her mind and continued on her way. The fish, like the stream, were long gone. She shook these thoughts from her mind and continued on her way. The fish, like the stream, where long gone. She still had the small sand dunes to get through before she reached home and it was getting late. Morgos always liked his evening nutritional time to be ready upon his return, and it was even more important that she not be late this time. He, of course, would be at the meeting for the men and, if needed, would put up his hand

and offer his help. This made her feel both proud and a little frightened. These new visitors may not be as pleasant as the last ones to come their way.

Anor reached her abode, got down on her knees and hugged her child. She looked up to her umnn's tae's child and thanked her for watching over the child.

"We are expecting visitors within the next two or three evening rest periods. We must start preparations to receive them." She told the other female adult what had been heard at the meeting and then the younger rushed back to her own home. She would have a meal to prepare herself and no one could afford to be late this time.

Each abode in the community was small and neatly organized, according to custom. The abodes were fashioned in such a way that an omn or umnn could see into each small room and keep an eye on a child, yet receive the privacy they needed. Anor was in the area designated for the preparation of nutritional times and was watching the child as he carefully constructed his idea of what a now long extinct household pet called a horath looked like. Remembering her history galaxy lessons of long ago, Anor thought how much a horath resembled an earth mouse except for the very long feet and tri-clawed toes; the feet themselves were almost an inch long. What made the horath unusual was its smell. It was almost like the animal had rolled in her flowerbed outside. A not too unpleasant smell to her and one that had calmed her enough to fall asleep many time in her own youth. It was an odour she would never forget and remember with fondness and love.

Her child would soon be learning these ancient lessons and hoped he enjoyed them as much as she had and that he would see the same similarities she did between the two animals. There wasn't much about the earth known to her planet, but what they did know, except about the animals, frightened them, both as children and as adults. She hoped it wasn't earthlings that were coming to visit.

The lessons she had been taught about earth centred on that planet's war history and her planet, Kladax, had always been one of peace. Only twice in its complete history had they gone to war, and each time it was because someone else had tried to invade them and never because they had shown the first signs of violence toward others.

She joined the child on the small floor covering and watched him play. This had to be one of the best parts of her revolution and she was reluctant to surrender it. But there were things to do. She slowly rose to her feet and went about them.

Anor had the evening nutrition ration on the eating platform when Morgos returned. He sat down and started eating quickly, something he never did. He usually took the time to play with the child about his waking time. Then, he would eat a leisurely nutrition and then get the child ready for his rest period. She felt there was a great deal about the news of visitors that he couldn't share with her and that was also new to her. Up until this period they had shared absolutely everything with each other. Having to keep things from her must be hurting him very badly, she thought, as she saw him to the door as he rushed off.

She then gave her first thought to the new ones in the community and wondered if they would be at the meeting. She turned and prepared the child for his rest period and as she did so her fears grew. After all, how much did they really know about the new ones? She, for one, knew so very little.

As she bent over the child to brush her lips across his head, she noticed he was already developing the small horn at the bridge of his long narrow nose that all males grew. This horn usually didn't start making an appearance until the child was at least three summers old and her child was barely two summers of age. They grew up so fast she thought as she finished putting the nutritional items away and went to her own resting platform. Her mate may be very late so she may as well get some rest while she could. She knew he would want to talk, if allowed, when he returned and that would mean a very sleepless time for her. Not that her imagination was going to allow her much rest to begin with.

Second Waiting Period

The room was packed with men ready to serve and the noise level matched that of the roaring crowd at the old games field when there were teams to use it. The Ruling Council Leader called for quiet.

"We are facing the most difficult challenge of this planet's history," he said. "The ship coming our way could be friend, or it could be foe. We don't know, so therefore we must make plans for both.

"Our watchers tell me there haven't been any friendly ships in our skies for some time but that does not mean they are not there. The same holds true for those we could consider enemies. Up until now we have not welcomed many visitors to Kladax but we have always tried to make the few feel welcome and we will do so again.

"However, if this ship holds enemies to Kladax, we must be prepared to defend ourselves. I will not allow this planet to fall into unfriendly hands just because we do not have a history of defence. Therefore, we are here during this rest time to discuss our defence, how it will be handled and by whom. I am aware, by your presence, that all of you are willing to take on this onerous task."

The cheers rose until not another sound could be heard. The Ruling Council's Leader allowed it to work itself to a natural conclusion and then regained order. He then asked for ideas from the floor as to the most efficient manner of defending their home world. A few hands went up and he called on the first one he saw. The overwhelming attitude of the crowd was, since they had always been a peaceful people, where would they acquire the weapons to fight, if it came down to it. There were people there from three generations before the newest that had never held, or even seen, such a thing. It was going to be a turbulent time ahead for everyone.

It was almost time for the sun to rise when Anor heard the footsteps coming toward her. She looked up and started to smile but the look on Morgos' face stopped her smile before it got a chance to start. She rose to a sitting position and waited for him to take his place at her side. His voice was calm and quiet, even for him. She felt a cold chill go down her spines. She was going to loose him to war.

"I am sorry I didn't voice you but the meeting went on and on."

Kissing his cheek, she told him she understood and it was all right.

"Are you in need of nutrition?"

"No. Sleep. Sleep is all I need. But thank you."

He fell back onto his headrest and was asleep instantly. She would have to wait until he rose to find out what he wanted to tell her.

She gently covered him with a sleeping cover and settled back onto her own head rest and fell asleep staring at her mate's crinkled face as he slept and dreamed something horrible enough to make him call out several times during the time. She slept with the dread of what he was going to tell her come first light.

The risen sun found Anor waking to the sounds of her mate pacing the floor in the next section of their abode. Their child, she saw, was sitting at the nutrition platform eating his nutritional allotment for this time frame and she joined them, rubbing the sleep from her right eye. She smiled at the two men in her life as she reached for some hot liquid. It was a liquid a space traveller had introduced them to several years before and it had become quite popular, even though it was most difficult to grow in their climate. The traveller had told them he had found it because of an interaction with the Mars colony that was destroyed in the last war. The earthlings had a strange name for this liquid that was totally unpronounceable in their tongue, so it was just called the hot liquid.

She had found she had become like her omn and enjoyed the taste of the liquid first thing in the morning and again during the mid point nutritional time. Morgos could not understand what they found so wonderful about it but he also did not try to get her to change to his favourite drink – the liquid from the pulverizing of the dew slug. It was quite sweet for first thing in the morning but exceptionally healthy.

"You did not sleep well, Morgos."

"I'm fine. There is just too much going through my mind right now. Besides, I wanted to spend some time with the child. I haven't seen as much of him as I like these past few revolutions." He playfully tweaked his child's chin, sending the small one into giggles.

"What are you up to during the mid point nutritional time?" he asked her while helping the child pour some liquid of the dew slug. The child had taken to it also and it pleased Margos.

"I will be making your child something to eat, as I do every rotation. Are you coming back to the abode for yours or will you be elsewhere?"

"I was hoping you could get someone to watch the child so we could have it together."

She thought for a brief moment and then nodded her head. She would call upon, once again, her umnn's tae's child to come over. Her betrothed was still away so it shouldn't be too much of a problem to bring her children over and they could spend the rest of the period together. It was something they didn't get to do all that often so it would be quite the treat for the children.

They agreed to meet at the nutritional centre at his building and he left to start his working time. He left her neither feeling at peace or with dread. That just made her worries all the stronger.

She spent the rest of the time she had to straighten up the abode and make sure there were enough nutritional choices for six in the house. It meant making an extra journey to the nutritional disbursement centre but it helped take her mind off her forth-coming talk with her mate.

He was waiting for her at a nutritional platform set for four when she entered the room. He normally would have chosen a little platform for two so she expected someone else to join them. She wasn't disappointed.

A few moments after she sat down, another adult male walked up to the platform and Morgos rose to his feet. This adult male must be someone from work, she thought, someone to whom he answered.

The adult male took her hand and tented it with his, as was the custom when meeting someone else's mate. He then took a seat and put a paper case on the platform in front of him.

How rude, she thought.   A male would never do that unless...yes. The two of them were going to discuss work. She started to rise to allow them to speak freely when the adult male put his hand up, motioning for her to take her place.

"I did ask you to come so we could have a discussion," Morgos said, "but I was rude in not saying it would be with another. I know how nervous these sorts of gatherings can make you, but it was important that you be here. Please forgive my rudeness." He looked to Anor with pleading in his eyes. How could she stay mad at him?

She regained her seat and assured Morgos she was not upset but, yes, nervous.

When they rose again, it was time for the two males to return to work and Anor had been sworn to secrecy about what she had heard. But she now knew what had turned her mate's sleep upside down. Her mate would not be going to war, but would instead be part of the group that led it and the ship that was heading their way was not one of peace but the dreaded warmongers she had heard about since childhood.

The Rnites were coming.

Anor spent the rest of the sun hours trying not to worry and this just caused her to worry all the more. She couldn't talk with anyone about what she knew and Morgos was at the Ruling Council office. The two of them had talked very little after the official from his office had left them and Morgos had promised they would talk after the evening nutritional time. What was she going to do until then? She started cleaning the abode like it had never been cleaned before and then she started all over again. Her umnn's tae's child had sensed her nervousness and had taken the children to play with friends and Anor had turned the voice machine to record. She didn't trust her voice not to give away her fears.

She was washing the walls in the sleeping area for the third time when her mate and their child walked in together. The others had returned to their own abode to give the couple time alone to talk.

Anor quickly fed the child and put him on his sleeping platform. Because of all of the hard play at the fresh air station, he was soon fast asleep, his favourite sleeping item hugged tightly to his tiny chest. She gently ran her finger over his new horn and then left him to sleep.

"Morgos, have you seen the child's horn?"

"Yes. It is wonderful, isn't it? But isn't it early for it to come?"

"Yes. But children develop at different stages. Remember, the child was late starting to walk but early to speech?"

"True," Morgos smiled. "We must have the naming ceremony soon. It is only right."

Anor became serious. "Do you think the Rnites will want to fight us? Isn't it possible they just need something from us and then they will go away?"

Morgos put his hands on her shoulders. "They do not behave in that manner, Anor. If the Rnites are coming, that means only one thing." He sat in his chair and sighed. "We can not wait until the Rnites leave to hold the ceremony. We will have it when the sun rises."

"Do you think they will be here as early as they say?"

Morgos nodded. "Yes. The scanners have them as being less than a full rotation away."

That meant they could be there as early as the sun.

"Oh, nuts." Anor had recently become a fan of old earth literature and had started using some of the slang she read about. Morgos found this habit anything but endearing but knew it was just a phase of self-expression she was going through. It seemed her omn hadn't allowed any slang, earth or otherwise, in the abode while Anor was being raised so she found herself using it when she discovered something new. The last time she went through this, the phase was over before the end of the seventh rotation. Morgos knew this one would last about as long. It was by far better than any of the other choices she had, he thought.

First Period of Conflict

"I wish to see the new members of our community as quickly as they can travel here."

The Ruling Council's Leader was assembling as many as he thought would be of help at this time of crisis and who better to ask than someone who had already fought the Rnites. They may very well have escaped by the vapours of their engines, but they had knowledge that may help their new homeland survive.

Grorth arrived at the Ruling Council's chambers and waited respectfully to be asked to enter. He and his crew had not been on Kladax long, according to local customs, but they had learned the manners and customs, and if they were unsure, they found waiting for instructions was the best thing to do. There were times that just walking in, even when asked, was taken as a slight and the last thing Grorth, or any of his men, wished to do was to insult their hosts. They liked living on this new world, had come to consider it their own and they did not wish to do anything that would necessitate their hasty departure.

The Ruling Council bid him enter and was told because of his situation, they would not be standing on ceremony. Grorth still waited to be asked to sit and once that had been done, the questions came at him like lightening.

"May I respectfully ask for one question at a time, Great Leader of the Ruling Council?"

Ashamed, the Ruling Council's Leader apologized and asked the first question of hundreds that Grorth would answer over the next quarter of a rotation.

When the Ruling Council had finished asking, Grorth was asked one last question by Morgos.

"Have you any idea why the Rnites have not just obliterated us like they did your home planet of Theasos, Grorth?"

Morgos and Grorth had become friendly over the past few revolutions and they each held a great deal of respect for each other. Even with that, there still remained a certain level of mistrust between the two.

They both found Anor quite beautiful.

"I have no idea, Morgos. If only I did. This is definitely out of what I know of as their normal practice. Have you been able to establish voice contact with them?"

The Ruling Council's Leader turned to the adult male in charge of the intergalactic voicing system and silently asked him the same question for the third time since they had sat down.

"Leader, my department sent out voices from the first time the scanners reported their presence. The only voice we received in return was one so profane that I did not consider reporting it. I, instead, chose to alert the Ruling Council of the Rnites presence and their history in each quadrant they 'visit'. I also informed the Ruling Council I would alert them to any communication from the ship at the instant it took place."

"As I would have done, Burmor, as I would have done." The Leader looked again at Grorth.

"It confuses us, as it must you, Grorth."

"Indeed it does, Leader. How far away are they now?"

The Leader checked his rather elaborate but very accurate timepiece. Rumour among those who worked closely with the Leader had it that his timepiece set the official time of the planet. True or not, it made for an interesting subject of conversation for those that would never get the chance to verify the rumour.

"According to this," he said, "less than three portions of a revolution. That is, if this time piece is to be believed." All of those present snickered accordingly. Almost to a person, they had heard it so many times before they were sick of hearing it and it was even less funny now.

"The one weapon we have to be careful of, if they choose to fight and believe me when I say they will, is a disruptor that can go through bulkheads without damaging them but killing their targets."

Everyone assembled in the room stared at Grorth as if he had suddenly grown a second head.

"I know. It sounds fantastic, but there it is. Apparently, this weapon was developed on earth and as soon as they realized how devastating it was, they banned it. All existing weapons were supposed to have been destroyed."

"Are you suggesting someone from earth gave the Rnites this horrible thing?" The question came from the lowest ranking member of the Ruling Council and someone who rarely spoke out, not only at Ruling Council gatherings, but anywhere. It took everyone by surprise to hear his voice but then they all recovered and waited for the answer.

"That is exactly what I am suggesting, Members in Good Standing." This response brought the room to silence once again.

"Did this human...?"

"No, Leader. There isn't any possible way the traitorous human could have survived."

"Thank Olag. Is there any way of detecting this weapon at all?"

Grorth thought for a moment. "The only way I can think to detect it, and please bear with me, I'm not an engineer or a propulsion expert, is to check for ion radiation trails. The way I am to understand it, the disruptor is powered by the engines, thus leaving its own trail in the engine emissions." He looked around the platform and continued. "Before you ask, I have no idea from there if I am wrong."

The Ruling Council all looked at Grorth with sympathy and the Leader thanked him for his input, and honesty.

"You have, even in your limited way, helped a great deal. Would any of your engineers or propulsion crew have any more to offer us?"

"I'm afraid not, Leader and Council. It is customary for the *schlimin* of our ships to know all there is to know about our own, but the knowledge of others is extremely limited to what they want us to know and unfortunately the earthlings were not too forthcoming with their knowledge unless it was something they needed assistance with at some point. For instance, we were the sole suppliers of nutritional supplementary replenisher parts for several years so we knew their systems inside out. However, once they changed their design, we were no longer 'in the loop' as they were known to say. I am sorry."

The Ruling Council's Leader was quick to say "Please do not apologize, Grorth, for what the earthlings did not share with you. However, can you think of any other way we might acquire this knowledge, and quickly?"

"I am afraid I do not, Leader."

"Then, so be it. We will check for ion radiation trails, then."

And with that the gathering adjourned. The Ruling Council agreed to gather in the communications room after giving that department time to try to raise the Rnites on the voice machines once more. Meanwhile, the engineers would have had a chance to check for the ion trail and anything else that may come to mind in order to see if the ship headed toward Kladax was a warrior or a scout ship, which some members of the Ruling Council suggest it may be. Outside of those few members, no one else held that hope in their hearts.

Morgos took advantage of the break and voice to his abode. Anor and Travor were entertaining his friends and their omns as a continuation of his naming ceremony and Morgos was disappointed not to be able to share in the excitement first hand.

"I am so sorry, Anor. Please tell everyone how much I wish I could have been there."

"Not to worry, my betrothed. I fully understand and Travor sees it as just a party at which he gets the most attention, that's all. As much as you don't really want to hear this, where you are and what you are doing is much more important than your child's naming parties, of which there will be many. You will not miss all of them, I assure you."

Morgos sensed rather than heard her sigh with that last thought. He knew only too well the amount of gatherings a naming ceremony could spawn and it really could be most exhausting, but the parents could not afford to offend anyone by turning down a single invitation. His heart went out to her. He just prayed her anger that she was trying, and not succeeding, to hide would abate soon, but as it was foremost in her words, he had serious doubts. He would have a great deal to make up when he returned to their abode. He really didn't need this impending violence from a force he had never seen before right now. He really didn't. Giving a sigh of his own, he joined the rest just as the communications director was starting to give his report to the Ruling Council.

"Leader, Council, I have voiced the approaching ship three times in the time allotted me and they have voiced back but once. I recorded that response. Would you like me to play it back for you at this time?"

"Please."

"As you wish, Leader."

The director reached over and turned two dials and the next thing everyone in the room heard was a bit of static and then a very deep voice came through.

"Our metal scanners tell us you do not have enough of what we are looking for, so you have been spared. However, these same scanners tell us you have a visitor ship orbiting your planet and wasting away. Would you please tell us from where this ship came?"

"Why?" the Ruling Council's Leader queried.

"We are looking for such a ship that we have unfinished business with." The recorded voice had left everyone with the feeling their question had been anticipated. The Leader looked at Grorth, who could only shrug. The director silenced the voice machine.

"This is true, Leader. The Rnites would enjoy killing me very much for eluding them all that time ago."

"I am sure they would, Grorth, but that will not happen in my space or on my planet." He had made a decision to throw aside thousands of generations of ingrained honesty in all things as he signalled the director to re-establish the voice link. He would do whatever he had to do to ensure the safety of his planet and all who dwelled on her. Taking a deep breath, he began down a road he thought he would never travel.

"I am sorry but I have checked the reports on that ship and they all read the same. The poor souls aboard did not answer our voices when they entered our space and we could only conclude that there were no survivors aboard."

"You did not transport aboard to verify your suspicions?"

"According to our customs of privacy and respect for the dead, that would have violated many of our religious and legal laws."

"Then we shall."

"Not while that ship is in our air space! I have just told you…:

"But we are not bound by your laws."

"That ship is in our space, so our laws prevail no matter whom else is here. You will leave that ship as she is."

"No one, including you, will tell us what we can, and cannot, do."

"If you so much as scan that ship, you will be blown out of the skies."

Laughing, the *duoman* of the Rnite ship voiced back. "I would love to see you try to do that! Many have tried and all have failed, including that ship."

The Rnites broke the voice and Grorth looked the Ruling Council's Leader straight in the eyes.

"Just how do you propose to do what you just threatened?"

"I have no idea. But I had to say something, didn't I?"

"The Rnites are not easily fooled, you know."

"Yes. I do."

"There may be one…"

"Leader!" The director's assistant shouted out.

"What is it?"

"We have visitors, Leader."

All eyes went to the side of the room behind them. Approaching, and bearing weapons unseen before by them all, was the strangest creatures that not even the most active imagination could have conjured up. There were three of them and they each stood only 1.2 metres high. Their heads were so large they seemed to be at least a third of their body length and their eyes almost glowed. Grorth couldn't help compare their eyes to the glow the old-fashioned radiation glows he had read about as a child.

But it was what they were holding that captivated the Council and Grorth's attention the most. If Grorth wasn't mistaken, the Rnites were holding scaled down variations of the outlawed disruptors from earth. Where had the Rnites got the technology to do that? he wondered. He, for one, didn't want to push his luck to see if these weapons actually worked or if they were just a bluff.

What Grorth was most concerned about, however, was the way the Rnites were looking at him. He obviously wasn't from this world and it wouldn't take the Rnites long to figure out who he was. He had to find a way out of here without loosing any of the lives of the men who had become his friends and allies. He waited for the Ruling Council's Leader to speak and then he slowly slid his hand over the console to his right and flicked open the voice system that went throughout the building. He never took his eyes off the invaders.

"He is…" began the Council Leader.

"We know who he is. Silence! We have found what we have come for." The three of them stepped forward, in step and as one, and without taking their eyes off Grorth, stopped almost nose to chest with him.

"You will come with us." Their voices were flat in tone and emotionless. It was as if they had learned to speak the language one word at a time.

"I don't think so." Same tone, same expression. Grorth was not about to back down from these killers, or allow them to see how truly frightened he really was.

The Rnite closest to Grorth turned his weapon slightly and let go with a burst that sent everyone into a shiver. The female who had just brought the liquids moments before the Rnites arrival suddenly disappeared in a very small puff of white smoke. The tray she had been holding landed on the floor with a crash, liquids of many colours pouring out of their receptacles.

Grorth took a tiny step forward and saw all three weapons trained on him faster than he could take a breath.

"You want me, you have me. But I ask only one thing of you before we go. Spare these men their lives. They haven't done a thing to harm you and they never will." He looked to the Ruling Council's Leader for affirmation. He got it. "I assume your ship can hear everything that is transpiring here?"

"So?"

"I just want the rest of your ship to know that I have cooperated with you, that's all. I don't want any misunderstandings about that."

"You are correct. My *duoman* can hear every little whine you put forward in your defence."

"Good. First allow me to inform you that the way you are facing is your number three mistake."

What the hell was he doing, thought Morgos, trying to get all of us killed?

"Mistake? Why is it a mistake? Are you not standing in front of our weapons, pleading for your life?" With that, they all snickered. They were obviously enjoying this very much.

"Your second mistake is to under estimate me. Or my men."

"I believe that is your mistake, not ours."

Grorth kept talking as if the Rnites hadn't uttered a word. "But your first, and biggest, mistake was to leave your home world at all." He hoped if he kept on talking an idea would come to him. For maybe the thousandth time in the course of his short career as a spaceship *schlimin* he wished he had had the training that the title required. Being a ship designer before the war gave him the knowledge to operate one but nowhere near the skills to command one.

"We have been in contact with other planets and they are sending us help as we talk."

"Do not try to deceive us. Be quiet and stop wasting our time. You and your crew will come with us. Now."

An idea suddenly came to him.

"If you had the power, you would already have us on board your ship." Everyone in the room stared at him. He was right, of course. Why hadn't the Rnites just transported those they wanted aboard their vessel and left? What was preventing them from doing it even now?

Suddenly the look of absolute terror crossed the Rnites' faces. They had had the same thought. For some reason, their ship had lost the ability to transport their prisoners, or anyone else, back aboard their ship.

"We are experiencing a small amount of difficulty at the present time." The Rnite ship had made contact and it had startled everyone in the room when the voice first came through. "Please stop badgering us and we will get the problem solved that much more expeditiously. Have I made myself clear, Su?" The voice from the Rnite ship was as panicked as those on the surface.

"Uh, yes Sir, you have, but that would be Ta, Sir."

"Not if I hear from you again, it won't be."

The Rnite stood and hung his head, then took two steps back. Not another word was spoken by any of the invaders, but the looks on their faces said it all. Whoever was in charge aboard their ship instilled more than just a little fear when under stress. Grorth wouldn't have wanted to cross that person, either. But the most astounding thing to Grorth was the way the three of them turned colours, from the most putrid shade of green to an almost gemstone colour of red. Amazing. He would have to investigate this phenomenon more another time. If he got the chance, that is. The only other creatures he had ever heard of doing anything closely resembling this were the earth's chameleon, some of their fish and his planet's mouse.

But foremost on Grorth's mind, besides the fear these creatures were able to create, was did his men get his unspoken message over the voice system? He pretended to sneeze in order to turn his head toward the door he needed to see, which was almost directly behind the Rnites. The shadow across the small coloured window told him they had. He silently sighed with great relief. He then turned back to face the enemy.

He may not be the most qualified *schlimin*, but he had won sneakiness competitions hands down his whole life. If truth be known and told, he thought, they could write a learning hologram on some of his victories from his misbegotten youth that had become legend on his world. It wasn't that he was dishonest, just sneaky. Then there were the times as an adult that brought smiles to his face to think about them.

But time for that later. He passed the signal he and his men had agreed on months before if they found themselves trapped and the door behind the Rnites opened slowly, quietly, and three of his best men crawled into the room on their bellies. Someone from the outside just as quietly pulled the door closed and the three made their way up to their intended targets. No one had heard a sound to this point.

They crept up to the three and each slowly rose behind their targets. Before the Rnites knew what had hit them, they were stretched out on the floor with their each of their heads sporting a large lump. Grorth's men had bashed them with the ends of heavy wooden mallets. The three sleeping beauties would be out for some time to come, giving everyone time to plan their next move.

Everyone in the room quickly rushed forward to help put the not-so-smart Rnites into a locked closet, after stripping their voicers and weapons from them, for the lack of a better place to put them, and secured the door. He pulled it off, thought Morgos. The crafty *theod* pulled it off. Kladax had been a planet of peace for so long jails had been unheard of for over a thousand years. There was someone available and ready to pose as the Rnite when the voice came, but the Ruling Council hoped to question the Rnites before that happened. Then, the Ruling Council and their guests returned to the Ruling Council chambers. There was much to discuss and no one was quite sure just how much time they had before the Rnite ship would try to reach their men again.

The ideas and opinions were flowing before the door was even closed and anyone had taken their chairs. But, none seemed feasible. Even Morgos, who had been called into this because of his planning and strategy abilities, could not conjure up a plan that was both sound and logical. Those assembled talked far into the darkness and some had fallen asleep where they sat when the voice from the Rnite impostor came through.

"Leader, the ship has just voiced down that it will be our sunrise at the earliest that they can transport even one person and their voice machines were going down, also. They only had one-way voicing so I was not required to answer."

Everyone looked at each other and smiled. They could not believe their good fortune. Without saying a word, they all stood and headed for the door. Each was hoping to be the first to ask the now sleeping captives what might be happening aboard their ship. If their thoughts were accurate, the Rnites would not have the power to transport anyone, even come the first rays of the sun. This was something all at the meeting were hoping for, and counting on. They hastily made their way down the corridor, all talking at once, and almost rushed to the closet door, with each having the idea he would be the one to wake the now not so terrifying or dangerous invaders. Any dignified or professional attitudes were cast aside in the excitement. Several hands shot out at once and made a grab for the door handle. In the confusion, a hand came from out of nowhere and gently turned the handle. The door swung open and everything and everyone came to a halt and all noise stopped.

It appeared, at first glance, that the captives were all dead. Not one of them had moved since being placed in the closet several hours before. Just as one of the men reached his hand down toward the one closest to them, the Rnites moved just the slightest bit, scaring the Sinspinner out of everyone. Then several hands went out to help the captives up and out of the small space.

After the Ruling Council and the Leader made their apologies, the illness and wellness officer checked them out and gave each one something for their headaches and put a poultice on the lumps. The Ruling Council Leader then started asking them a few simple questions.

"Why would your ship be experiencing all of these difficulties getting you back?"

The Rnite who had been acting as the leader since transporting down differed to the smallest of the three.

"When we became space worthy," he began, "the designers of the program put everything the weapons systems and next to nothing into the rest of the ship.

"They told the Monarch that the ships would last two life times and then some. Well, our ship is only half a life period old and already almost all of what other species would call 'basic things' have started to fail.

"On our way here," he continued and looked right at Grorth, "our life support systems started to fail and we had to discontinue the nutritional growth program in order to obtain the liquids it was using and put them back into service for us.

"Therefore, it comes as no surprise that the transport systems have failed. They run off the electric systems and we have been at half-light for weeks.

"It was part of our Monarch's plan to allow you to rescue the prisoners so we wouldn't have to feed or house them any longer and then we were going to take your ships. But the earthlings put up a much larger fight than we had planned for and we had to destroy them.

"The ships that were part of that battle never made it home. We are still looking for our comrades and we will never have the ships that it will take in time.

"We only guessed that you were here because this is the first inhabited planet within range and we were only a bit surprised to see you here. We were, however, most surprised to see your ship in such good repair after all of this time.

"I am sure that if you were to surrender it to us, the Monarch would let you live."

He stared at Grorth as if Grorth's answer depended on his living. Grorth's heart went out to the captive, but he really didn't know what to do or say. The Rnites only wanted his ship in order to continue to kill and he just couldn't live with that.

"I think I know what you are thinking about us," the captive said. "We truly only want your ship in order to find our men and return home. We are tired of killing and destroying planets for such a small return of cerium. We, the crew but not the officers, have accepted that our world is going to die. There is a time for it no matter where you are from or your personal beliefs, and our time is now.

"Please believe me when I say we mean you no more harm. I know I am not leaving this planet alive so why would I tell you a falsehood?"

The Ruling Council's Leader assured him that if it were in his power, they would all leave alive and well.

"You don't understand. We may be transported back aboard the ship, but we will be vapourized for allowing ourselves to be captured alive. That is a worse crime than any other to us. They won't even allow the transport to conclude. We will be vapourized while our molecules are floating in space. We die, no matter whether the transporter fails or not."

"What will happen to the rest of the souls aboard your ship if they do not acquire mine?"

"Then they will not have the power to return home. They will be condemned to space and eventually die."

The whole room was so quiet they could hear the night birds calling to each other on the other side of the gap in the wall that they used to see outside. The night birds had only a trill for a call and it was so quiet in the room it was if they were all together, side-by-side, birds and beings. The thought that those aboard the spaceship would be condemned to die a horrible death in space was one they would rather not contemplate.

Out of the quiet came a tiny voice asking the most profound question, one that all had thought but none could put into the air.

"If we could find a way of getting them here, why not bring them down? We have room for them all." The voice was from Morgos and he had been just as intimidated about asking as all the others. He now waited for either the laughing or the shouting to start. He was disappointed on both fronts.

After a lengthy silence the spokesman for the captives said, "We volunteered to transport down because we had no intentions of going back. We knew it was only a matter of time before we lost voice with the ship and then we had planned to ask if we could stay. But please believe me when I tell you that there aren't many like us on that ship. The rest would rather die a senseless death in space than admit the Monarch, and all the Monarch's before her, was wrong or that it was time for a change of attitude. They would all follow the lead of the *duoman* and he would stay with the orders he was given, no matter what, because he wouldn't want to appear weak to the others by accepting your offer."

"Then what would you suggest we do in order to save your friends lives? Transport aboard the ship and forcibly remove them? Follow them through space until they come to realize we are their only hope and they give themselves up to us? Wait for them all to die and then bury them in a strange place on a strange planet? Please tell me what we are supposed to do, because for the life of me, I don't know."

"We," he said, looking at his fellow crewmembers, "appreciate the fact that you and your populace are a peaceful race and only wish to do what is best for my fellow Rnites, Leader, and we also appreciate the fact that you didn't kill us when you had every chance to do so. But when it comes to a Rnite soldier following the orders of his commanding officer, there is no subordination allowed whatsoever unless you can do it in such a way as to never get caught. Even what the three of us have done is unconscionable to everything we have been taught and raised to believe. Being sneaky is one thing, but getting caught at it is another and just being here and talking with you can, and will be, taken as an act of treason."

"But how would they ever know what transpired here unless one of you three informed on yourselves?"

"Please make yourselves comfortable and we will do our best to tell you what volunteering for a mission away from the ship means and what must happen before those who are leaving actually transport down." The Ruling Council and guests sat back and waited. They were not prepared for what they were about to hear.

"Please do not assume that we three just put our hands up and we were transported within a few minutes. First, we reported to the medical unit, where they implanted a tracking device under the skin of our necks.

"Then we reported to operations control where the devices were checked to make sure the operator could see us on the screen at all times.

"Next, we were taken back to medical where we were subjected to a truth answering drug to make sure we had not volunteered just to avoid more hazardous duties elsewhere.

"Then, the tracking devices were armed with a small, but very powerful, explosive device that could be triggered in an instant if they thought we were not being loyal.

"After that, the doctor kept us in a drug-induced sleep, where the mind control officers made sure we knew exactly what we were supposed to do and nothing more.

"When we awoke, we were questioned for two revolutions of time without sleep or any other comfort to assure absolute certainty that we would not break under torture if we were captured in a hostile environment.

"After being allowed half a revolution of natural rest, we were transported down here."

"How in the name of Olag did you manage to conceal your real reason for volunteering after all of that?" The Ruling Council Leader was dubious and incredulous.

"Believe me, Leader, it was not easy. It took many bribes and much sleep learning to be able to lie effectively and then to get it all past the doctor. That was the real challenge, so we voted amongst ourselves and chose one speaker for the three of us. I lost, or won, depending on how you see all of this, and I was the first to volunteer. Then, after waiting a few hours to make it look as if their actions were one of support only, the other two stepped forward and said they would accompany me on my mission so I would not be alone. They only had to have the tracking devices implanted and armed and they were ready to go because it was my mission, alone, and they were, in effect, only guards to make sure I performed my functions properly and returned to the ship in a timely manner.

"As you can see, it was anything but easy to get here and then tell all of you the real reason for our visit." He paused for a moment and then assured the others the armed device would have been made safe when the ship's computers started malfunctioning. "The tracking devices, and the armed heads, were controlled by the ship's computer systems and without them, nothing can happen. In that respect, you are safe."

"I am so sorry we treated you so shabbily. It is not in our nature to resort to violence and it has actually become a crime to show any ill will toward anyone at any time. How can we possibly make it up to you except to welcome you into our society and make sure your every need is met?"

"Please, Leader, you did what was necessary in order to protect yourselves and your populace. Let it pass and do not worry any more about it.

"Now, shall we put our minds and hearts toward something of more importance than that?"

"Yes. We must find a way of saving your friends and still allow them to retain their dignity and maintain their rituals. Let us call for nutrition and get to work. Grorth, would you be so kind as to ensure the required nutritional needs of everyone is met?"

"It would be my honour, Leader. Leader, may I have your ear for just a moment before we begin? I know it is not customary, but I feel what I have to say is important and for your ears only at this time."

"Of course."

The two of them stepped into the hallway and Grorth swallowed hard before beginning. He knew what he was about to say was, in many ways, totally foreign to Kladaxions and he knew he had to word it in such a way as no one could possibly take offence.

"Leader, I am sure my words are unnecessary, but..."

"Grorth, if you are trying in your most mannerly way to say that all of this could be a trap and exactly what the Rnites are up to, rest easy my new friend. I have lived in a peaceful society all of my life, but that has not precluded me from learning from other societies and their methods of achieving what they want. Many societies have used deceit and I am ever watchful for it. I may not be an expert, but I believe I have always had the ability to see it in the speaker's eyes and so far I have not seen it. But, as I said, I am always watchful.

"Now, Grorth, please make my nutrition as bland as possible. Unfortunately, one of the effects of all of this emotion is a not so happy stomach." Laughing lightly, the Ruling Council's Leader rejoined the group.

Grorth walked over to the ordering voice, still very much worried that the Ruling Council's Leader was not truly aware of all of the dangers in what he was about to do and asked for the nutrition to be sent. As far as he was concerned, they were still very much at war with the Rnites and he planned on acting accordingly. He took a moment out to voice his abode that he most likely would not make it back until after the next sunrise. He then joined the others. Reading about something and actually seeing it for the first time for yourself were two totally different things and Grorth felt the Ruling Council's Leader was about to find that out.

The Ruling Council, Grorth and his men, along with the three Rnites, spent the rest of the dark period working out how they were going to get the remaining Rnites to come to their senses and transport down to Kladax. When no one could continue without rest, they adjourned for the period to refresh, have nutrition and see family and friends. The three visitors were asked if they would like to see parts of the community after a rest and they agreed. Grorth decided to accompany them. They agreed to meet after the mid nutritional period.

Second Period of Conflict

An eighth of a revolution later, a small mixed group of home worlders, new comers and visitors set out to visit the attractions the area had to offer. Grorth and five or six of his crew were there and seemed to any observer to be a happy portion of the assembly.

They took in the usual parks and recreational areas provided for the use of all and then they saw one or two of the same kinds of areas that had been set aside for the Ruling Council's exclusive use. It was explained to all that sometimes members of the council had to have an area where they could take their families and friends and not have to worry about the general populace begging for favours as is what sometimes happens in the common areas. Each of the members was always so busy that was the only way some individuals could get an audience and they didn't hesitate to take advantage of it. No one on the Ruling Council blamed them. That was just the way it was.

Next were the governing buildings that were public accessible and the museums that had been built in the old court building. They toured the old prisoner restrain areas and the vapourization unit. The Ruling Council's Leader took great pride in telling everyone about the last time the unit had been used.

"It was exactly one thousand years ago this year," he said. "The prisoner had accidentally killed his neighbour and the law back then stated that even in accident the person responsible for taking another life other than animal had to meet his death, also. That period, or day as it was called then, there was an uproar from the crowd gathered outside and they made the Ruling Council of the day see that by taking this male's life, they weren't any better than he was, if not worse. It would have been a legal murder that was all.

"So if anything like that happens since then, we take pity on the poor soul who takes another life and rehabilitate him back into society as one who has had a horrible experience instead of one who has done a grievous wrong. But, thank Olag, that has not happened in my life period and I am of substantial age." Everyone nervously laughed at his small joke. A male must have reached the age of at least sixty summers before he could even apply to sit on the council and then must sit for another twenty or so before qualifying for the position of Leader. The reigning Leader had been in that chair for some summers already and showed no signs of leaving.

Grorth thought back to what an earthling had told him long ago. Given the same time frame, the earthlings were just devising new and more painful ways of killing each other while Kladaxions were trying its best to do the exact opposite. His own Theasos had ceased killing one another in just the last one hundred years. What we can learn from one another he thought as they left the building to return to the visitors' lodgings. But then again, he thought, one thousand years ago we were still living in caves and trees. "I guess we have really come a long way in a very short period of time," he whispered to himself. Then he looked to see if anyone had heard him. His crewman standing next to him had and nervously but knowingly smiled at him. Grorth took that to mean that they had had thoughts alone the same lines.

The Rnite ship tried twice more during the break time to communicate with their men on the surface, but each time the voice was broken through no fault of either side except inept equipment. The Ruling Council and the rest of the planners worked with everyone who had expertise in voice communication to try to make the failing system work, but to no avail. It could not be done from the surface.

The Rnites had been in Kladax's space system for three periods of time now and had managed to communicate once with their men on the surface and that voice had been interrupted.

One of the younger technicians who had boned up on the basic knowledge of the Rnite system offered to transport up and see what he could do from there but all, including the visitors, were concerned that he would be killed upon arrival. The Rnites aboard the ship had no idea the workers would be arriving with peace in mind and to help, not sabotage. Until they got some sort of voice system up and running, there wasn't any way to tell the Rnites what had been suggested, let alone planned. But come what may, they were determined to save the lives of the stranded Rnites if at all possible. The big challenge was keeping what they were doing from the citizens until they knew if they could actually help the Rnites without putting anyone in immediate danger. Keeping something like this a secret in such a close community was going to be difficult, so speed was in the forefront of everyone's mind.

Morgos excused himself and returned to his office so he could work quietly and with as few interruptions as possible. He had acquired a huge headache from all of this and he felt totally useless standing around the meeting room talking about things that would never work. He closed and locked his door before heading over to his workstation and getting down to business. From what he knew about Grorth, he could count on him to get and keep order.

For the first time in his working career, Morgos failed to turn on the building voicing system. He just couldn't have the conversations from the other room interfering with his thoughts right now. It was one of those rules of the building that had been passed into law for all government buildings and was done automatically with severe punishment for those who failed to comply. The main reason for this law was because the voice system was the most efficient means of giving vital information, such as life saving warnings, to those working inside the buildings and thus achieving the maximum results with the minimum amount of effort.

Morgos was sure with all of those with higher ranking than he on the council busy elsewhere, no one would notice and even if they did, he would be able to bluff his way around it by telling them why he needed complete quiet. He was sure he would get away with it.

Meanwhile, the Ruling Council and the rest of those assembled two floors above were working feverously trying to get some sort of message to the stranded ship. Time was running out for those aboard and as the clock ticked, they were that much closer to loosing the fight to stay alive.

The Ruling Council's Leader asked the visitors if they knew the code they were in need of, but because the three had been assigned to species identification only, they were of no aide.

"Grorth," the technician asked, "would you happen to know what the Rnite's coding for emergency would be?" Each planet had an agreed upon system for broadcasting emergencies in space that was supposed to be registered with the Galaxy Members office but since Rnos had not joined the Membership, no registration existed.

"I have no idea but they must use one that would be able to be recognized by others, you would think. How many are on the registry?" As an unqualified *schlimin*, he had not memorized the registry or any of its components as the fully trained had to do before getting their commands. "Could they," he ventured, "actually be using one from the registry itself?" He felt a bit silly asking, but it was always a possibility. You couldn't trust the Rnites not to pull any kind of illegal stunt.

The technician went over to the computer that held the Galaxy Members issuances, such as their constitution and laws. This computer would not accept any information that was not generated by the Membership. Each registered planet had such a computer and took the best of care with it because one and only one would be issued. If the computer crashed or malfunctioned in any way, it was the duty of the assigned planet to replace it and the only way that could be done was by finding another world that would allow their computer to be cloned and that left their computer open to many different invasions that could destroy it;   so not that many planets were willing to participate in such a venture.

The technician entered the required key codes and then voiced in his security codes by using an enclosed voice receiver that recognized not only his codes but also his voice patterns. All of this took several minutes and everyone waited patiently because they knew there were only a very few with the authorization to use the computer. The last thing he did was to scan in his own security measures which were his fingerprints from his left thumb and right pinkie finger. Each operator of the computer was required to input this extra measure and the only choice they had was what they wished to use for their addition to the program. Some used voiced dates, some used key codes and some used pictorial entries. All were acceptable because only the computer knew what each individual used.

"I have the list on the screen, Leader."

"Good." The Ruling Council's Leader was very impressed with the ability of one so young. The technician, he thought, could not have seen more than twenty summers, if that many. "Now how long will it take to work out which one, or combination of those registered, they use?"

The technician was hesitant to answer but he swallowed and said, "It could take a few portions of a portion of a revolution to a many revolutions, Leader. There are hundreds of registered signals and codes and they could have used any one of them or theirs may not have anything in common with any of these. All we can do is try."

"How will you know if you have found the appropriate one?"

"I will program the computer to transmit each combination and we will be notified when the signal has reached their computer, whether they have the capability to answer or not."

"Get started."

"Leader."

The Ruling Council's Leader did not mean to sound as harsh as that tone came across as it was considered rude and the technician did not take it as an affront but as the tone of a being experiencing extreme frustration and anxiety. The success of this endeavour could mean that not only would the Rnites live, but everyone would also be spared the final journey to meet Olag, a trip the technician was not ready to make at this point of his young life. He had not seen his twentieth summer yet and he planned to see at least the same amount his umnn's umnn had seen – one hundred and thirteen.

"Shall we allow...I am sorry...I do not even know your designation label. How do I address you?"

"Leader, do not be sorry. You had no reason to know my designation label. I am addressed as Druith."

"Druith. That is a strong and valued designation label." Turning to Grorth, the Ruling Council's Leader explained. "Druith was a fine leader in his time. He was a member of the council that forged our new laws and constitution that led us to be a planet of peace instead of conflict. If you remember, his likeness hangs above the access to this building."

"I do remember," said Grorth, "it was one of the first stories I heard after arriving here. Druith is the reason all of you are who you are." Using his voice with great emphasis and strength was not him talking down to the young man but instead he was showing how this young technologist's name source had impressed him. There weren't many stories like this one on his home planet and he was both impressed and jealous, but he wasn't about to let anyone on Kladax know that. He just didn't have it in him to tell his new 'family' his home planet was almost devoid of emotions. They would never understand what that felt like for someone with emotions, and he wasn't about to explain it to them and bring something that painful into their lives when it wasn't necessary.

"Shall we allow Druith to complete his work in peace? Meanwhile, as we await the results of his search, we shall adjourn to our abodes for nutrition and relaxation until we are voiced to return. Morgos is hard at work on a plan to deliver our signal when the time is right and there is no requirement keeping us here until we are summoned."

The Ruling Council and its guests stood outside of the building, saying their salutations for a restful period when the building itself gave a very small shake. Each turned and faced the structure in time to see it settle back onto its foundation. No one was able to speak for some time and when they did their voices were filled with fright.

"It could not have been a ground shudder as all of the other buildings are as they should be." The Ruling Council's Leader was the first to find his voice. "We shall enter and each search a floor, reporting back here as quickly as possible." Turning to one of the lesser members he asked him to stay outside and make sure the rest made it out safely. The member quickly agreed because he knew what an honour it was to be responsible for the lives of the Ruling Council. He took his post eagerly. Because no one knew the stability of the building, or what had caused it to shudder, those gathered to watch could do nothing but wait outside with the guard.

The rest entered the building and stood just inside the door. "Announce which floor you are searching and go quickly." Several said they wished to accompany the Leader but practicality demanded they take a floor of their own. After all, they had thirty floors to cover and only twenty-three searchers. The visitors had been asked to wait outside for the time being. Grorth took two and ten of his men volunteered to take extra floors. It took only moments to sort out who would take which floors and they were on their way. Grorth started for the basement and the Ruling Council's Leader went for the mass conveyors and the top floor which housed the Ruling Council chambers and other meeting rooms, along with the computers and other machines that allowed the government to function.

The Ruling Council's Leader must search the top floor for one reason only – if the computers had been damaged in any way, only those with the highest clearance would be allowed into the room. All entries would have been automatically sealed and only those with the highest security clearance would know the codes needed to reopen them. The final code required was known only to the Ruling Council's Leader and he had to be assured no one would have a chance to see him enter it onto the key pad. He would then change the code as it could only be used the once. If the code was entered again for whatever reason, such as the unheard of act of terrorism, the computers would seal the building and no one would be allowed to leave or enter for two periods. The small entryway to the mass conveyors, once the weight of anyone trying to enter a conveyor was sensed, would be flooded with nitrous oxide, putting the interloper into a deep sleep until they were rescued and arrested. They then would be vapourized without guilt assessment because of their obvious responsibility.

Anyone working on the floor at the time of the attempted illegal entry would then be released and most likely ignorant of what had happened, since the Ruling Council did not have to publicize such things and everyone employed in the government buildings were taught their first day to leave immediately and ask no questions when the alarm sounded. Only those on the top floor would still be there when the building was accessible once again.

Until this period, all of the Ruling Council's Leaders had thought this precaution frivolous and silly. Now, the present Ruling Council's Leader was of the thought to have even more security added to the process. It all depended on what he found when he gained access to the thirtieth floor.

Morgos felt the building shake and immediately made his way to the main entrance. There he found the volunteer left behind by the search party.

"What happened? I felt the building shake and ran like the Sinspinner."

"We do not know at this point, but the Ruling Council and their guests have gone back inside to do a search to find the cause. All we know at this point is that it wasn't a ground shudder because none of the other buildings here have been affected. Please stay here and wait for any others who may still be inside to exit. I am taking designation labels so we will know if there are any workers missing."

"What can I do to help?"

"Crowd control may become necessary."

"Thank you, Councillor Morgos. If you would be so kind as to set up your post on the other side of the entry we will be able to check the citizens as they come out and maybe put them into groups, such as from which floor they emanated or maybe which division in which they work, and then we will be able to tell if, Olag forbid, anyone who is supposed to be here is missing and we can send someone in search of them. Does that make sense?"

"Your organisational skills are excellent. Shall we begin? I believe I hear the first ones coming."

"I thank you for your insight. If anything has damaged the thirtieth floor, the visitors will be directly affected and all possible communication with their ship may be lost for the time being." He looked at the anxious visitors and relaxed. They were not to blame for anything that may have happened. They could very well have been victims, also; if there were any in the end.

"It is not traditionally a full work period so the amount of workers will be limited." The guard got back to his duties quickly. There would be time to reflect on everyone's role in whatever happened later. His duty at the moment was clear and he would carry it out to the best of his ability.

"Agreed."

The first wave of workers came through the door as they spoke and they were processed very quickly. The next group took some time due to the amount but they, also, were assigned their waiting areas in an expeditious manner.

The minor member of the Ruling Council and Morgos were processing the third, and much larger, group when they heard the shouts from the voice machine. The words coming through were almost unintelligible but someone did get that someone had either seen or had found something that was horrible.

A voice from the gathered workers called out. "That voice sounds like the Ruling Council's Leader's voice." The worker who spoke sounded nervous to mention his thoughts but he went on. "I have had the privilege of working with the Leader and it does sound like him. Where is he supposed to be?"

The minor member of the Ruling Council told everyone the Ruling Council's Leader was on the top floor, making sure all was secure and safe. Someone pointed and called out to look. There, on the image machine, was the Ruling Council's Leader staring down at them. Terror was written all over his face and he hadn't stopped screaming.

Everyone made a mad dash for the entries and it took everything Morgos and the other male had to restrain them and assign two members of higher ranking on the Ruling Council to go to the Leader's side. Protocol stated that the rescuers must be of top ranking in case there were governmental secrets uncovered and left out in the open. Two of the crowd stepped forward, presented their designation label chips, placed them into the identity machine and entered the building. Meanwhile, Morgos sent for the medical division to be ready at both the entry and at the medical building reserved for the Ruling Council and their staff, located one plot of property away.

The voices of concerned citizens came to an abrupt halt when the two Ruling Council members were seen coming toward the door, helping the Ruling Council's Leader. They had him by the arms and it was quite clear that he needed them to help him walk. His face was still contorted with fear and his tears streamed down from his already red eyes onto his ceremonial robes.

The sea of beings parted to allow the three to pass unhindered and enter the small transporter designated for the Ruling Council. Small scatterings of subdued and concerned conversations were heard as the entry to the transporter closed.

It was shortly after the transport was completed that Morgos remembered those working on the top floor. He turned and made a mad dash for the entry and didn't stop when called. Grorth caught up with him as the door to the mass transporter was closing. They took it to the top floor and stopped dead in their tracks.

The entry to the floor stood open and the devastation inside was one Grorth had only heard about from ships he had fought alongside against the Rnites. They had used their weapons that allowed them to pierce the walls, leaving them intact, and kill their targets.

The dead and their blood covered the floor. As Morgos and Grorth looked around, they could see very little actual flesh left. It was as if those caught by the beam of the weapon had exploded from the inside out. It reminded Grorth of the nutritional item he had left in the warming system too long and the beams had destroyed it.

They stood, staring at the carnage and said a silent prayer to Olag, then turned and slowly left their friends behind. They said not a word to each other on the way back down. What was there to say?

However, each was deep in thought and Grorth couldn't help thinking, sadly, that he had been correct all along. The Rnites had tried to set a trap for these poor, peaceful beings and when they had not fallen for it, had taken their shots at anyone in the room, innocent or not. What would they do when they found out they had missed their prime targets - Grorth and the three messengers they had sent to their deaths – and, instead, killed twenty souls not connected to their fight? Something told Grorth the Rnites probably wouldn't care.

Morgos and Grorth arrived at the entry and stopped. Morgos had the sad duty to inform all those assembled of what they had and it wasn't going to be easy. The closest he had ever come to sharing sad news was when his tae's pet *schlink* had died. She had only had it a few rotations and was still trying to decide what to name the creature when Morgos discovered an ancient textbook that taught his ancestors about the wildlife of other planets. He was thumbing through it when he came across a picture of a similar creature to his tae's and the book had identified it as a Tricon III rodent and an earth rabbit. There had been some small differences, but not enough that it stifled a laugh from the small children to discover three different planets in the far reaches of the galaxy with basically the same animal. Sadly, the poor thing had not survived the first winter and his tae had refused any other pet from then on. She had cried for rotations and went into a deep withdrawal that lasted, in many ways, to this very rotation.

True, there were many differences between sharing the sad news of the death of a beloved pet and the murders of fellow workers and government officials but the emotion was the same; grief was grief. Morgos steeled himself for the duty that had fallen upon him and took one last deep breath. He was grateful Grorth was there with him to help answer the onslaught of questions that were bound to come.

"My fellow citizens," he began in the ritualistic manner. "It has fallen upon me to" and he had to catch his breath. He didn't trust himself not to break down with tears. Grorth gently placed his hand on Morgos' elbow. Morgos gently nodded and continued. "It has fallen upon me to report the murders of all who were working on the thirtieth floor of this government building." He got no further.

Citizens were shouting out their grief and questions all at once. It took the complete Ruling Council to bring things under control and then to make sure everyone's questions and concerns were met and answered. When things were finally done and the citizens had returned to their abodes to grieve, the Ruling Council, Morgos and

Grorth silently re-entered the building to begin the official investigation and remove the remains of those inside.

Grorth had tried to beg off as being an outsider but the Ruling Council would not hear of it. He had been there when the murders had been discovered, he had done battle with the Rnites and he was the closest Kladax had in an expert in murder. None of the Ruling Council had ever heard of a murder in his life period and didn't know where to start. Had this been the murder of one of their own by one of their own, they would have formed a law regulation group and left it to them. But it wasn't. It was a slaughter of several of their citizens by another species and there wasn't a protocol for dealing with anything close to it. Grorth heard the logic of their arguments and agreed to help. If he thought he was in over his head as a *schlimin*, he was definitely out of his depth as a murder investigator and if he wasn't mistaken, this was actually a declaration of war. He sighed and then went to join the others on the thirtieth floor. Just when he was starting to think his days as a warrior were over.

Morgos stopped at his office on the twenty-eighth floor and found the ancient book written about the last murder on Kladax to use as a reference guide. The book was so old he had to turn each page as if he were touching the wings of a delicate *bruttlalea*. He went on up to the top floor and joined Grorth at the entry to the floor.

"We know the designation labels of everyone here and we know the designation label of the species who committed the atrocity. We even assume we know why they did it." Morgos stopped, as if it took everything he had to continue with his thought. His heart really wasn't into investigating the murders of some of his closest working friends and associates. All he wanted to do was hand it over to someone else, but he knew he couldn't until he had charted the room. The book that he took his guidance from told him that was one of the most important things before allowing anyone else into what they called 'the crime area'.

"All we really don't know is what they plan to do when they find out they failed in killing their true targets," Morgos said while wondering how they were going to punish those who had committed such a crime.

Grorth felt sure he knew what they could expect but kept his opinions to himself. He hated the thought that he and his crew had brought this devastation upon such a peaceful and caring planet. He would have to live with it for the rest of his life, however long or short it may be and still thought he was getting off easily.

"My biggest duty will be to notify the families of these poor souls of the deaths of those they loved. Then I will have to obtain a list of volunteers who will be willing to come up here and clean. That will be both the easiest and the most difficult thing I have ever done in my life. Everyone will feel they must volunteer for the duty but I must only allow those who have the internal workings for the work and for the life of me I don't know who that would be. We have never had an incident in which everyone on this planet in living memory has had to put their bravest foot forward until today.

"The medical unit will, naturally, take care of the bodies and then see to it that the burial unit takes it from there.

"I would like to close this floor for perpetuity but it is not feasible. We are already stretched for space as it is and the loss of this floor will cramp everyone beyond endurance. I will, however, see to it that it is designated a special area of memory and all who enter this floor will pay homage to those who lost their lives here today. I just hate to think we may have to make this sort of investigation unit permanent."

Grorth looked at his friend and asked what made him think along those lines.

Hesitating for a few moments, he explained. "It's just a bad feeling I have. I know the Rnites won't stop here once they realize you and the others still live and because of that we may have more deaths to deal with. I pray to Olag I'm wrong, but I do not think so."

Grorth couldn't answer that but did think Morgos could have come up with no better tribute to those lost than to have the whole floor as a tribute, but he also hoped Morgos was proven wrong. He hoped to have the remaining Rnites off that ship before they acquired the knowledge their targets still lived and had time to plan another attack.

Mapping out the location of the few bodies that were identifiable and the areas the rest had come to rest had taken many portions of a rotation and they were both sick to their stomachs and exhausted when they were finished. Morgos said the prayer for the tragically dead and Grorth said his for the souls lost in battle. Grorth found it rather more than a coincidence that both prayers called the dead 'brave soldiers of life'. He had noticed several things that closely resembled the life on his beloved Theasos and the prayers were the ones he chose to mention to Morgos.

He waited until they were ready to leave the building and then phrased his thoughts in the gentlest way he could because, after all, he was still speaking of the dead.

"Morgos?"

"Yes, Grorth. Let me venture a guess. You have noticed the similarity in our departing prayers for those of yours."

"Yes."

"Let's stop in my office once more, shall we? There is something there I think you would like to see."

They entered the office and Morgos went directly to an elevation device that allowed him to access a book on the top shelf of a massive bookcase that ran the full length of the room, ceiling to floor. He gently removed a volume from its place and put it on the table behind him. He opened it to a page close to the start and turned it slowly so Grorth could read the script.

Grorth read the words slowly, twice, and then looked up to see Morgos looking back at him. Grorth was not as amazed as he was gratified in his thoughts being confirmed.

"Is this fact or just one writer's opinion of what may have happened?"

"Fact. The book itself is only three hundred years old but the author gleaned the story from old files and personal family stories. It seems his ancestor was part of the migration after some sort of catastrophe. Do you remember anything along those lines from your history lessons?"

"Certainly. We were taught that there had been a terrible war and our world was covered with fallout from the bomb that destroyed the surface. Some of the survivors went underground long enough for the air to clear and the rest went out into space." Grorth stopped there. Could it be? Could Morgos be a descendent of the same populace he had spawned from?

He knew from his lessons that his ancestors had thought about going to earth but did not find the living conditions suitable to their needs at the time because earth had barely come out of what was later called the middle ages and the inhabitants would never have been able to grasp the concept of space travel so they had gone on.

Theasos had lost touch with them after several portions of an orbit as they went out of range of their primitive voice machines of the era and did not learn where, or if, they had settled. As to the thought that they could have landed up on this planet, anything was possible, Grorth thought. Anything was possible.

"We may be able to get along and work together today because somewhere back in the past our ancestors knew one another, or maybe were even related. What a thought." Morgos found the thought rather nice, actually, and smiled his agreement. To think the original inhabitants of Kladax and Theasos may have come together and created a new species Grorth now knew as his friends. What a thought.

Morgos and Grorth left the building together and stopped outside to see the first rays of the sun and to wish each other a peaceful rest period, what was left of it, and agreed to meet for the mid point nutrition time.

"I still don't see why you are requesting my help, Morgos. I'm an outsider and have little or no influence on your citizens, as it should be."

"Oh, how wrong you are, Grorth! After you told your story and how bravely you fought the Rnites, just to have them show up here, your knowledge is invaluable, my friend. It is my true belief we cannot defeat these invaders without your help and guidance. Sleep on it, Grorth, and you will see I am right."

Grorth's upbringing would not allow him to enjoy and agree with the ego rub Morgos was giving him, but it was something for him to just hear it.

They both had a great deal to think about and Morgos had to finish preparing his presentation to the Ruling Council. Grorth remembered reading in an old earth book that someone had said 'war is hell' and he couldn't have said it any better. The Sinspinner was having a good laugh right about now and Grorth was determined to see that that laugh was short lived. One way or another.

He returned to his abode and fell upon his sleep platform, too exhausted to sleep. He lay there with his hands behind his head and went through the events of the hours since the last sun. He was starting to wish he had not brought the ship to this tiny planet and most of all he wished he had not accepted the inhabitants offer for a new life amongst them. He could not change what had happened, but he sure as Sinspinner could make sure it didn't happen again. Maybe Morgos was right after all. Maybe because of his battle with the Rnites, he did have an insight into them that would be of help to these citizens.

He jumped up from the sleep platform and activated his voice machine. When he had completed the calls he had to make, he fell once again onto the platform, but this time he slept the sleep of the ....pardon the expression....dead.

Third Period of the Conflict

Grorth and Morgos met at the arranged time and place. Morgos had voiced the Ruling Council and asked them to meet him in the Council Chambers before the mid point nutrition time for a quick discussion.

"I am interrupting a Ruling Council gathering. I shall…"

"You shall step inside and take a seat, Grorth." The Ruling Council's Leader gently pointed to an empty seat. He was still recovering from his fright on the top floor a few rotations earlier and each of his movements showed his inner pain. He was not the Leader he once was and it pained everyone present to watch him so full of fear. However, they also knew it was, hopefully, only a matter of time before his recovery was as complete as it was going to be, please Olag. "We are here because of you and it would not be polite to continue without your presence."

How formal, thought Grorth. Why? He took his seat as requested and waited. The Ruling Council's Leader then spoke.

"Morgos, holder of the fifth seat to the right of the Ruling Council's Leader, speak."

Something definitely strange was happening here, thought Grorth. In all of the time he had been on Kladax, never had he heard such formal language. True, this was the first official gathering of the Ruling Council he had attended; he could tell it was an official gathering because they were all wearing their Robes of Office and if that hadn't told him, the sign at the entry had announced it all. But still.

He knew it had to be serious, but those robes. They were absolutely ridiculous! Purple and green? Who came up with that?

Grorth suddenly realized Morgos was talking. Pay attention, he chastised himself. This is important; critique the choice of clothing later.

"So, Grorth, the Ruling Council agrees with me that you would be a valuable asset to this planning unit. Would you allow us the privilege?"

What? Oh, yes. He had asked me this when we last met. He wants me to help come up with a strategy to defeat the Rnites. I really don't want to be that involved. I just want to get the Sinspinner off of this planet and leave these poor souls alone.

"I would be honoured, Ruling Council." *What?!? Did that come out of my mouth?* He couldn't believe he had said that.

"Thank you, Grorth. We are honoured. You will work with Morgos on this and the two of you will give your final plan to me and to me alone. Gathering closed." The Ruling Council's Leader had a great deal of his old self back, but everyone knew a great deal of his manner was still a façade and that he was having a great deal of difficulty keeping it up. He was the first to leave the room for the first time in anyone's recent memory. No one commented on this but went about their business. There was a lot to get done in such a short period of time.

The Ruling Council's Leader had made it official. Grorth was to sit with the planners and help them defeat the worst enemy in the universe and he couldn't even keep his own crew safe. What a joke this was turning out to be.

"Morgos? Morgos, we have to talk. And now." Grorth knew his tone of voice and choice of words could, and would with most citizens on this planet, be construed as an insulting address, but he didn't feel as if he had the time to be all that polite. Morgos had put...No, he had put himself into a situation he didn't want to be in and he had to find a way of getting out of it, and quickly. He wasn't capable of helping these souls no matter what he had thought earlier and he would most likely just end up making things a lot worse than he already had just by being there.

Morgos turned and faced Grorth with a shocked look, but he quickly changed his expression to one of questioning. He knew his friend was frightened of helping them and he did not mean to offend, but he really was the only choice they had to use as an experienced consultant. He also knew he had to help Grorth see that he could help, but Morgos had to finish talking with the holder of the Ruling Council's third seat from the left first. This male held a great deal of power with the rest of the Ruling Council and Morgos could not afford to offend him. He accepted the member's glowing praise of him but managed to cut it off just short of total embarrassment, which was difficult for a citizen of Kladax since their custom told them that no amount of praise was embarrassing. It was a sign of change for the populace as a whole for those that felt that rude emotion.

There were many subtle changes happening to the psyche that, when taken one or two at a time, meant nothing, but put together in groups or all together, meant the citizens of Kladax were slowly evolving and changing. Today Morgos felt embarrassment at receiving compliments and not long ago a co-worker was on the receiving end of a rude comment and to it in stride, explaining to the speaker that he found the honesty stimulating. Now he was having to convene a group of cleaners to go through a murder scene and not feel anything. What was next? An approval for the war they were fighting? The thought of it scared Morgos more than he cared to admit.

He joined Grorth as quickly as he could and started to apologize for keeping Grorth waiting.

"Not to worry, Morgos. Your conversation with an influential member of the Ruling Council, or even the one who cleans the Ruling Council's Chambers, deserves your complete attention. Our conversation can wait that long, surely?"

"You are too kind, my friend. I sense your words were what your omn taught you, not us." He offered Grorth a small smile.

Returning the smile, Grorth admitted to the source of his manners. "Omn made sure we were all fit to be taken out into society by the age of two and believe me, if you had been raised by Omn, you would practice those instructions by second nature by the age of three." He and his twenty-three siblings had been raised without any input from their umnn, as custom stated, but all of them knew their umnn could, and would, put his foot in if needed and that scared them more than anything their omn could do. A healthy fear of one's umnn was not necessarily a bad thing, Grorth mused.

"Your omn sounds like a female adult after my own heart." Morgos' thoughts went to his young son, waiting at home for his return. Anor was raising his son with a set of values that seemed to Morgos, at first, to be rather extreme but after meeting and getting to know Grorth, Morgos could envision his son in twenty summers making his parents proud because he would be able to handle himself in any situation on any planet he might find himself. Morgos smiled at the thought.

"Enough talk of omns for the moment, Grorth. We have work to do and abodes to get back to. Shall we get started?"

"That's what I wished to speak with you about, Morgos. I don't feel it is my place to..."

"I know what you are trying to say, Grorth," Morgos interrupted. Again, he was finding himself doing things he would never have done just a few short revolutions ago. "You and your crew are the only ones here on Kladax to have even come close to the Rnites, and because of your war experiences, you know basically how they will behave." Opening the door to his office, he then said "Now shall we get started?"

Grorth knew when he had been beaten, but he also couldn't find any argument so he just nodded, smiled and entered the office. Whatever help he could be, he thought. "Let's."

The two of them closeted themselves in Morgos' office and asked not to be disturbed under any circumstances, short of an actual attack by the Rnites.

"What do you think would be the ideal way of getting their attention but without them thinking it as an act of war?" The frustration sounded in Morgos' voice and Grorth felt for him.

"Do you have space buoys in your arsenal of greeters?" He was remembering the small ship that went out to greet his when it arrived. The ship held a group of three lower government appointees and they had presented Grorth and his crew with small gifts of welcome. Maybe, just maybe, there was an unmanned ship they could send up with a message of peace.

"We used to have something like that. Let me make a few voices and find out."

When Morgos said 'voices' it reminded Grorth of the ones he had sent while at his abode earlier. He motioned to Morgos that he was going into the other office for a moment and hastily left the room. He reached for the voice machine and reached all three of his crew in the same room, waiting to hear from him.

"We have assembled the crew and are waiting for further instructions, *Schlimin*." They knew better than to ask what had taken so long for him to get back to them.

He explained what had been happening since he voiced them and asked them to have a little more patience with him. "I believe our mission is about to change." He joined Morgos with a neutral look on his face and took a seat at the work station, ready to work.

They went through the ideas submitted by the Ruling Council members and disregarded them all. Some were so ludicrous that they didn't even finish reading them. One of the members had suggested they send a ship up with surrender flags all over it and when the Rnites boarded they could be ready with party favours and food. Morgos offered that he, for one, didn't plan on dying with a piece of *traanfl* in his hand.

It took them the better part of their work time to weed out the useless and get to the possible. It was another work time that did not end much before the next sun and lately there had been many of these.

Morgos and Grorth literally fell into their respective sleeping platforms and slept the sleep of the just. However, if anyone were able to eavesdrop on their dreams, they would see just how unsettled they really were. All Morgos could see were laser hits all over the planet and he was helpless to stop them. Grorth saw everyone being herded onto the Rnite ship and as soon as they went through the portal they were turned into snarling creatures.

Each nightmare reflected each dreamers worst fears and Grorth's was a reflection on the state of the warrior they had tried to save from the penal planet. A strong mind gone to waste had not honour or logic and he was deathly afraid whatever scheme they came up with would be too little and too ineffective to overcome the Rnites and they would all become slaves to them.

Morgos, on the other hand, had taken a page out of history and it had been the creation of the laser that had brought down more than one planet and the Kladaxions had put their weapons down before they developed the much stronger phaser. If the Rnites did decide to transport down Kladax would not stand a chance. The strongest weapon they could stand against an invasion with had the equivalent power to the decay eradicator the dental medical unit had used on his tooth on his last visit.

Both Morgos and Grorth tossed and turned and were back at their workstations periods before they were due. Neither spoke of their nightmares but they had a definite influence on the work output for that session.

Fourth Period of Conflict

Morgos had not forgotten to turn his voice machine on and he had an ear open for messages on the success or failure of communication attempts with the ship. The two of them were ready for a small break when they heard a voice come out of the voice machine.

"Morgos?"

"This is he."

"This is Borgon from the Communications Unit."

"Yes, Borgon?"

"We have established a very weak voice with the Rnite ship and it won't hold long."

Morgos and Grorth were half way across the room when Morgos voiced back they were on their way. They arrived on the fourth floor that served as the temporary home of the Communications Unit and found Borgon pacing the floor like an expectant umnn, which in actual fact he was.

"What took you so long?" He knew immediately he had spoken more from frustration than anything and apologized.

"No need, Borgon. I understand the tension you are working under." Morgos walked over to the console and saw what the team had put together.

"What was the last you heard from them?" he asked as he looked at the amazing jungle of wires and other items that, at the moment, he couldn't begin to put names to.

"They have run out of food pellets and their air is very thin. Their supply of water has depleted to almost nothing along with their gravity control."

"Can I speak with them?"

"You may get a message through, if you hurry."

Flipping the voice channel switch, Morgos spoke slowly and distinctly in case the Rnites interpreter control was also malfunctioning.

"This is Morgos, member of the Ruling Council of Kladax."

"..is..is...ther of ...e Ren... ship....."

"We would like to help you."

"….ine, ju... oo... ick...."

"If I am correct in what you have said, you wish us to help you. Is that correct?"

"Ye.."

"Good. We will send a small three-man ship up to you."

"...an... u..."

Turning to the male on his left, he said, "Get that ship ready to go. Now." The male ran from the room, yelling into a voice machine attached to his shoulder mount, giving orders to have the ship ready for flight immediately. He knew it would be ready when he reached the launching area. His men had never heard the order to prepare the ship with such force, but they were well trained and would never do anything other than ordered, no matter how strange the order may seem. Second guessing was out of the question and never would have occurred to any of them.

Then Morgos addressed Grorth. "I just hope we aren't being set up for an ambush."

"Me, also." Grorth knew what the Rnites were capable of and couldn't help but feel they were, but he didn't want to put any more pressure on Morgos than he was already feeling. With half of the Ruling Council either dead or missing and the Leader still not able to take full control, if had fallen onto Morgos and he was ill prepared for it even during times of total peace and tranquility. He was bright, very bright, but leadership to this extent had never been part of his plans, or training. Grorth would keep his thoughts to himself for the time being, and hope he would never have to voice them. "Me, also."

The ship was launched on time and they voiced back a short while later to say they had arrived and the Rnite ship was in darkness and not responding to their hails. The outer skin of the ship looked as if they had had an extremely rough journey. There were phaser scars everywhere and the rest of the skin was burnt and almost useless.

Morgos and Grorth looked at each time and wondered where to go from there. One could not just walk up to the spaceship's door and knock. Could one.?

"Why not?"   Morgos asked. It was as if he had been reading Grorth's mind.

"Why not, indeed?"

Morgos turned and spoke into the voice machine. "Try tapping the side of their ship with yours. But be careful. We don't want any rupturing to happen to your outside shell."

"Are you crazy?" the answer came back. "Sir."

It took a moment for Morgos to wipe the smile from his voice before answering. It wouldn't do to have the underlings hear him laughing right at that moment. "I may very well be, but try it anyway."

There was silence for a short while and then the ship responded. "Yes, Sir."

Everyone in the room held their breaths as they heard they distinctive sound of metal hitting metal. The small messenger ship tapped three times and then waited.

There was no answer.

They tapped three more times.

Still no answer.

They tapped one last time.

"We are returning home, Morgos. There is no answer and no evidence of life aboard."

"Very well. You gave it a good try. Thank you."

Severing the voice connection, Morgos then turned to Grorth and asked him what he felt the next step should be.

"I have to be honesty with you, Morgos. I am as lost on this whole thing as you are, but it would be my first thought to somehow verify they really are dead and then see what we can do to give them an honourable burial."

"Let's see the visitors and ask for their guidance on their burial rituals and see if it is feasible to do a proper ceremony and burial."

"I agree. This is something we just can't go guessing about."

While Grorth went in search of the visitors, Morgos went to the Ruling Council's Leader's office to report their findings and decisions.

"Leader, I wish to inform you of what has transpired and what has been found."

"Thank you for your speed. Report, please."

When Morgos was finished, the Ruling Council's Leader sat with his head in his hands and his elbow resting on the workstation in front of him. He had taken a posture no one with manners would take in front of another, but he was overwhelmed. Even with all of his knowledge and training, he had not been prepared for invaders in his space or for their demise while here. How was he to ask his citizens to board that ship and transport the bodies to the surface of Kladax for burial when he wasn't even sure all aboard were really dead? It could be trap and he could loose his equally untrained, and more than likely even more frightened, citizens on what would end up being a suicide mission. He had to find a way of verifying the deaths before he went any further.

He sat back up and faced Morgos, looking him directly in the eyes. "Morgos," he said, "we have a problem and I don't know what to do about it. I don't expect you to have the answer, either, but maybe between the two of us we can find some solution."

"I am at your will, Leader."

"Thank you." Taking several moments and even more deep breaths, the Ruling Council's Leader put the problem to Morgos bluntly.

"We have to ask the citizens of Kladax to send volunteers up to that ship and bring the dead back down here."

Morgos instantly informed the Ruling Council's Leader of what he and Grorth had already done in that direction and then said "If we do send a ship up, I, of course, will be aboard."

|No!" The Ruling Council's Leader almost shouted. "I am sorry, Morgos. Please forgive my ill manners, but this whole thing has me very much on edge. I will demand only one thing of the volunteers and the being that they must be single. I don't want to run the risk of loosing an umnn of small ones. I hope you understand, Morgos. I appreciate your braveness and willingness, but it must be this way."

"I forgive you, Leader, and I also appreciate your kindness to the families of Kladax, but this is something I feel I must do." He paused but kept his eyes on the Ruling Council's Leader's eyes. He had to make him see how much this mission meant to him. "I have come to know the three visitors of late and it means more to them than I can say to know the final happenings to their shipmates and leaders. I must, for their sakes and the sake of our budding friendships, to help them say a proper goodbye to these men. I hope you understand, Leader. This isn't just a whim I am acting upon, but true devotional duty to three new members of our society and friendship ring."

The Ruling Council's Leader was almost brought to tears with the sincerity of Morgos' words, He had no choice but to leave the final choice up to the citizens and hope for the best that all would return.

"I thank you for your honesty and loyalty to the citizens of Kladax, both old and new. Please make the announcement that volunteers may put their names forward as of this moon and we will try for first sun.

"May I also respectfully suggest you speak with your betrothed about your plans. She may have something to say about all of this and you just may not like what she has to say. But take her words to heart and do what you feel you must."

"Leader."

"Please do not think I am trying to lead your joining, but having been joined for many, many revolutions the one thing I have learned in all of that time is I must take my betrothed's advice and feelings into heart and find a way to make us both happy but also do my duty to the Ruling Council and the citizens it serves. I, of course, have never been faced with the severity of this situation or its choices of actions, but putting that aside, your betrothed and other family members must be in agreement for you to join the mission or you will be in the communications room along side of me. Have I made myself an enemy to your feelings, Morgos?"

"Of course not, Leader. You only have my future, both on the Ruling Council and in my abode, in mind and I thank you for this. I will, of course, consult with my betrothed and other family members and if they agree I shall be with the others at first sun. If not, you will find me at your right hand."

"Thank you."

Meanwhile, Grorth was having his own difficulties with the visitors. He had found them sitting around the nutritional platform in one of the community's better nutrition stations, enjoying a local dessert delicacy that should have brought smiles to their faces, but they were sitting there with frowns instead.

"Does not the *voltro* agree with your palates or was the complete nutritional time unpleasant?"

The visitor who had come to be known as Bloux looked up without a smile. He also did not invite Grorth to join the nutritional platform, as manners would dictate.

"We have been informed that your Ruling Council wishes to bring our shipmates down to the surface for burial. Is that not so?"

"Yes, it is, but only if it meets with your customs of burial and grief. I am here, actually, to discuss just this matter with all of you, if you wish."

The three visitors visibly relaxed and invited Grorth to join them. Each stood up until he had found his seat and then returned to theirs.

"We are sorry, Grorth, but we misunderstood the intentions of the Ruling Council. We did not understand that our feelings or customs would be considered at all and that was most upsetting to us. I am sure you can understand that."

"Of course I do, as does the Ruling Council's Leader. That is why I am here, to see what we can do for you and your shipmates that would allow those that have perished to rest."

The three visitors stared at Grorth for a few moments and then broke out into smiles, which was nice for Grorth to see. They then, as a group, relaxed and to down to the business at hand.

Grorth left the nutritional centre with a full understanding of the requirements for burial and headed straight to the Ruling Council's chambers, where he expected to find Morgos and the Ruling Council's Leader. He was told, however, that the Ruling Council's Leader had gone to his abode for a rest time and Morgos had gone to his abode to speak with his betrothed.

Grorth decided to take this time for his own nutritional time and returned to his abode and a cold repast. He hated preparing nutrition and usually only did so when an empty cooking chamber forced him to do so. He was almost finished his nutrition when his voice machine announced an incoming message.

"Grorth here."

"Grorth, I am sorry to interrupt your nutritional time but I must speak with you as soon as I can." Morgos was sounding quite anxious, thought Grorth. He would, of course, put his friend before his nutrition and responded to Morgos' request calmly. Whatever Morgos had to say, it was clear to Grorth that it had him quite distressed.

"Would it be convenient for you to meet me here, or would you prefer for me to come to you?"

It dawned on Grorth with those words that he had lost a great deal of his world's speaking patterns and had adopted those of Kladax. He was of mixed feelings about this but would work it out later.

"If you would be so kind as to join me in my abode?"

"I will leave immediately, Morgos."

"Thank you."

Grorth returned to his nutritional platform and stared down at his food. The thought of ingesting what he was seeing turned him completely off and he turned and walked away. It was an offence to the Great Olag to waste nutrition but Grorth felt he had no choice. He would leave the nutrition on the platform until his return and then he would dispose of it due to its condition. He would make amends to Olag by way of personal sacrifice by going without nutrition for a full revolution as called for by Theasos tradition. It was a sacrifice he had always found extremely difficult to do and therefore it had been some time since he had imposed it upon himself. The only thing that would pass his lips for the next revolution would be clear liquid that had been taken from the flowing *clava* behind his abode and allowed to sit out until it reached the same temperature as his abode. Just the thought of it made him shudder. He had never been that fond of clear liquid at any temperature but warm was the worst.

He left his abode and walked the short distance to Morgos and Anor's abode. He always enjoyed his visits to their abode and the best part was getting to play with their little Travor. He would stop along the way and purchase a naming gift for the child and present it to him with full honours since Grorth had had to miss the ceremony. It would please the child to have the attention and it would please Grorth even more to lavish it upon Travor. Grorth had thought many times if he were fortunate enough to have a child he would like him or her to be like Travor. A child with manners and intelligence would please any parent, but one who also took to instruction and discipline as this one did was rare indeed. Grorth had never heard of a child presenting himself to a parent and admitting to a wrongdoing before it had been discovered until he met Travor. The memory of that brought a smile to Grorth that was still upon his lips as he rang the announcement bell.

Travor opened the entry and jumped for joy at the sight of his favourite visitor. He had a smile on his face that told Grorth that he had missed the adult male as much as Grorth had missed the child.

Following Travor into the common area, Grorth presented the gift to the child.

"May I present you with this small symbol of your reaching the naming stage of your life. I hope it brings much pleasure to you in the coming times ahead." He then handed the child the small offering and stood back.

Squirming with excitement the whole time, Travor reached out and received the gift with politeness but extreme desire to know what the container held.

"Thank you, Grorth, for the kindness you have shown in presenting me with this symbol of your respect of my new stage of growth."

Perfect. He hadn't missed a single action or stumbled over the required words. Many children could not do this without help from a parent and he had even remembered the small step backward after taking the parcel in both hands.

Both giver and recipient then gave the final bow and they smiled at each other.

"Go now, Travor, and open your newest symbol. Do not make a mess and, if you wish, your parents would delight in sharing your happiness later. We must first talk with Grorth." Morgos could hardly contain himself because he wasn't sure of whom he was most proud – his child for remembering the custom of receiving they symbol or his friend for going to the trouble to learn it. Grorth was indeed becoming a true member of this society, Morgos thought.

"Yes, Umnn. Thank you, Grorth."

"You are welcome, little one. If it pleases you, we shall spend some play time together later."

"It would please me very much." With that, the child ran into his play area and fell to the floor, pulling the top off of the container as his little bum landed on the cushion that had been left there earlier.

Laughing, the three adults turned and entered the working area of the abode. This was the only area that had an entry that could be closed but they left it open so they could listen for Travor.

Grorth took a seat closest to the door and the other two chose seats next to each other on a long seat that Morgos had build.

Morgos began. "Grorth, I wish to volunteer for the mission at first sun and the Ruling Council's Leader has requested that I speak with Anor and other family members before doing so.: He looked at his betrothed and the smile that passed between them held great pain. "My betrothed has graciously allowed me to attend the mission but she also has a request. That is the reason we have asked you to meet with us."

"Anything I can help with would be an honour."

"Thank you. Anor?"

Because the request was Anor's, custom stated that she be the one to present it to Grorth. She knew she could trust him with her life but she wasn't sure if she may be stepping too far by what she was about to ask.

Nervously, she spoke. "Grorth, what I have to ask is most unusual and therefore it makes me a bit nervous."

"You can ask anything of me, Anor, and you need not be nervous. You are as a tae to me. I wish only to help you be safe and comfortable."

Anor felt a small droplet fall down her cheek and dangle from her chin. She had heard the words that she had hoped to hear and it pleased her. She ignored the moisture on her face and continued with her request.

"I thank you, Grorth. What I require is for you to stay with Travor and myself during Morgos' absence and to be here if I need you."

Grorth knew what was meant by her words and stood. He walked over to the other two and crouched low. Placing his hands on hers, he gave her the words he knew she had to hear.

"Morgos, it would give me great pleasure to ensure the safety and happiness of your betrothed and child during your absence. Please allow me this small token of my affection for your family and respect for your abode." He never let his eyes wander from those of Anor so she could see his sincerity.

"We accept your gracious offer of protection and happiness is ours in doing so." Morgos then stood and offered himself in bonding to Grorth by taking a step forward. Grorth rose and accepted this bonding by also taking a step forward. This brought the two of them together with toes touching. They gazed at each other's eyes and allowed them to be read for any falsehoods they may betray. When neither found any, they stepped back and then relaxed. The offer had been presented and accepted with honour and everyone could now focus their attentions and efforts on the coming sun.

Fifth Period of the Conflict

The announcement brought many forward but only three would be allowed to go because of the size of the small ship that would be used. The hopeful were standing around waiting for the first ten to be announced and then for them to be reduced to five possibles. Out of those five would come the three to climb into the ship and try to transport aboard an alien ship to whatever awaited them. Everyone anxiously waited to hear their names called had accepted the possibility that they would not return from space and had signed their oath of knowledge.

The Ruling Council's Leader addressed those assembled.

"First of all, I wish to inform all of you how brave the citizens of Kladax find each and every one of you assembled here today.

"The mission three of you will be undertaking at first sun will propel us into a new era. It is the hope of the Ruling Council that it is a new beginning toward two worlds coming together under an agreement of friendship.

"However, if it should be that those aboard this tiny ship find themselves facing an atmosphere of hostility, we on the Ruling Council pray for Olag to see all concerned through their time of struggle and safely back where each belongs."

With that, he called forth the first ten.

Morgos was disappointed not to hear his name called. Anor was pleased to no end but did not show it, for she knew how much being on this mission meant to her betrothed.

She gently put her arm around him and hugged him close. He gazed into her eyes and no amount of frowning could hide the pleasure from her eyes. He put his arm around her in return and understood her feelings. He had known all along that she had agreed with his going on this mission for one reason only and that was to please him. He loved her so very much and now his love for her grew tenfold. He gently led her away from the gathering and took her and their child home. If he had had to explain his emotions at that precise moment, he would have had to be honest and say he wasn't all that disappointed not to go. The thought he may never see his family again was more than he could bear.

The three chosen for the mission had their names posted on the society voice notices and the numbers at their departing party were in the hundreds of thousands. Citizens from all over made the trip and each carried the well wishes of their areas with them. Had it been possible, the Ruling Council's Leader thought as he gazed out at the assembled in the square from his office high up in the building, all would be present at this momentous occasion. But reality took control and those that could not attend sent their faith messages with those that could. The messages conveyed the thoughts of success of the mission and the return of all who ventured out to bring the victims of an unnecessary conflict back for final celebration and rest.

The party went on throughout the dark period and into the first rays of the sun. Those still there walked the three to the ship and bid them a fond farewell and best wishes for a safe return. It brought to mind to those old enough to remember the last time the citizens of Kladax ventured out into space and it filled them with pride. Those who had been aboard the ship that had knocked on the hull earlier were there and each was wishing he had been chosen once again. But duty and danger must be shared and they realized this. They sent up the loudest cheers as the ship left its moorings and headed out to face the unknown.

The crowd watched as the ship slowly disappeared and then it dispersed. Some stayed as close to the outside voice machines as possible while others returned to their abodes and workstations to listen there. Those that had travelled great distances to see the event were invited to join those who had abodes close by or to make themselves comfortable at the community recreational building not far away. Grorth made sure he was with the visitors at this time. The Ruling Council's Leader assured everyone they would not miss a thing.

The citizens tried to go about their tasks but of course they found it very difficult to put the thought aside that the may just have seen their fellow citizens and friends for the last time and they were responsible.

It was shortly after the mid point nutritional time that the first message came from the ship.

"We have reached the stranded ship and all is in darkness. Two of us will transport over and see what has happened. We will leave the voice open for all to hear."

For the next few moments, all that was heard was space static and then the sounds of footsteps could be heard.

"Leader, citizens and friends, we are on the bridge of the ship and there does not seem to be anyone here." Silence followed for a few moments and then the voice returned. "We have found the system the Rnites used to view the entire ship. How do we utilize it?"

The three visitors were more than quick to inform them how to turn it once and see into each area of the ship without leaving the bridge. "Turn the yellow knob on the left side of the view screen and then flip the three switches on the right, but be careful you flip them all together or they will stick and automatically shut the system down. After that, turn the yellow knob back to its starting position. The view screen should come on."

"Thank you." The voice from the ship had a sound of relief to it, maybe because with the view machine he would not have to go from area to area in person. Only he knew why and those that thought about it tried to put themselves into his place. No one was willing to say they would not have minded going from area to area.

"We have found two still alive!" The shout from space shook everyone. In the first place they had not expected to hear a shout and in the second the last thing the expected to hear was word of survivors. This, indeed, was wonderful news. "We have transported them to the ship and they will be returning immediately."

Everyone watched the landing area for the ship and converged on it in a swarm to help get the passengers off and into the medical transporter. The ship was back in the air in less time than it took to get the medical transporter activated. The two who had remained on the Rnite ship let those on the surface know when the ship arrived back and the first of the dead had been put aboard.

The transfer of the dead went on for some time and no one had returned to their abodes or workstations. They had all stayed to help in any way they could and someone had started the Kladax prayer for the dead. Everyone chanted the Ceremony for the Dead and then a lone child from the group approached the visitors.

"How do you honour your dead? I wish to learn."

Everyone and everything came to a stand still and a hush fell over the crowd.

Bloux knelt down to get face to face with the small child and held him gently by the small shoulders. Moisture was falling from his eyes so hard at first he couldn't speak. When he was able to go on, his voice was so quiet no one else heard what he had to say but the child.

"You have honoured me by asking and I wish to honour you by teaching you." He stayed squatting until after the two of them had shared a smile and then Bloux slowly rose and took the child by the hand and walked to the raised platform used for special occasions. He picked the child up and led him through the chants, prayers and toasts and the child repeated each along with him.

At the end of the ceremony, Bloux placed the child into the arms of the umnn and slowly walked away. He had been truly honoured and it touched him. His men slowly followed him back to his abode and they stayed the rest of the revolution, talking about those they had lost and wondering if they would ever see their home again.

When the last of the dead had been brought to the surface, the Ruling Council had a gathering and decided they would ask Bloux and his friends for permission to destroy the ship. The Ruling Council realized it was the last link they had to home, but they also knew it was going to become a hazard if they just left it there, slowly orbiting around the planet. It was at that time that they decided to seek out Grorth and ask if they could also remove his ship. It was not a decision they came to lightly and it wasn't going to be the easiest thing to ask, but ask they must.

Sixth Period of Conflict

The Ruling Council welcomed all to their chambers and began the gathering with the customary prayers that saw the dead into their first reward. The visitors then offered up their final prayers for the souls of the dead. It was most moving and the complete Ruling Council hated to have to follow it with the business at hand, but they had no choice. The Ruling Council's Leader spoke. It was obvious by his voice that this whole affair was taking its toll on him and he was in dire need of rest.

"Friends, we have asked you here today to speak of something you may find cruel or just plan unforgivable, and for that we apologize but we must talk of what is to become of the two ships that orbit Kladax." He looked at each and every one of the outworlders who were now part of this world and its society. He could tell that some of them had already guessed what he had to propose and some did not take it well. This he understood, because once their ships were gone, so were the last links to their worlds. It was not going to be an easy decision, no matter which way they went.

"We on the Ruling Council," he continued, "have given this much thought and because of the deaths on the Rnite ship, we believe it will become a health hazard to Kladax when its orbit deteriorates. It is the feeling of the Ruling Council we have no choice but to safeguard everyone on the surface, so we must seek your permission to destroy the ships. I am truly sorry."

The three surviving Rnites looked at the Ruling Council, had a short conversation amongst themselves and then the youngest and lesser ranked, named Jloorst, rose and asked permission to speak. It was granted with great enthusiasm.

"Ruling Council, Leader, members of Council, assembled citizens. I have been asked to speak to the request of destroying our ship. I thank you for the opportunity to do so.

"It is the feeling of the three of us that the Ruling Council is correct and to destroy the ship will be to destroy the last link we have of our own planet. However, because of our being welcomed here and made a part of your society, with full trust and honour, we are willing to have our ship destroyed in order to protect those we have come to call our family. All we ask is that we be allowed to return to the ship and try to send out one more distress signal and see if we can raise our home world once more."

"We, the Ruling Council, have discussed this also and find that to be a very reasonable request. The ship will be ready to leave whenever you are."

"We, the visitors turned members of your society, thank you and even though religion was outlawed on Rnos many generations ago, that does not mean we all stopped believing and therefore we ask Olag to protect you."

"Thank you."

The tiny ship departed the surface and many were there to watch it go. Some had wondered if the misplaced Rnites would set the charge themselves while they were up there and others wondered, if they did, would they come back before it discharged. There were many mixed feelings about how the three Rnites actually felt but the common consensus was that no one would want to be in their shoes with nowhere to really call home anymore; even those who had never really warmed up to having the Rnites on the surface stayed and wished them well. It seemed they had made more friends that they realized and would be missed by them all if they chose not to return.

"Leader, we have set the charge for you."

The voice came through loud and clear and even those who half expected it held their breathes to hear what followed. They all hoped to hear one thing.

"We will be returning now."

A collective breath was released and they prepared to welcome the visitors' home. They would have to wait until then to hear if contact had been made. Many hoped they had not and that door was now closed. Others thought it would have been nice to say a final farewell to their populace. The discussion was still going strong when the ship came in for a landing.

The entry opened and the three of them exited. They stood on the top step and looked down. "It is good to be home," the called Codid said. Everyone had their answer, no matter which side of the question they had been on.

The dark period was approaching quickly and the next sun would see the burial of all those who lost their lives in the building explosion. Everyone went to their abodes and prepared for the official grieving.

The Ruling Council had discussed the burial of the Rnites and decided to have their official burial the following sun but one. Grorth and two of his crew would go up and set the charges on their ship following the last ceremony

Seventh Period of Conflict

The sun saw the whole community and many visitors from other areas assembled for the burial ceremony and no one had to call for silence when the Ruling Council came out of the building to lead the procession.

The Ruling Council took their places on the raised platform, waited for everyone to find a spot where they could see and then the Ruling Council's Leader stepped forward.

The ceremony was lengthy and those who had lost their lives were honoured with story and song as the true heroes they were. They had gone to their workstations that work period and had not returned to their loved ones through an unprovoked and unforeseen attack of war. They were places in their tombs and the Seals of Honoured attached.

The Ruling Council and its Leader then stepped back onto the raised platform and waited for silence.

"This sun we embark on a new life on Kladax. A life of remembrance. A life without those we loved. But also a life of preparedness.

"As a gesture of this new way of life, it is my pleasure to reintroduce myself to you." The citizens didn't know what to make of their Leader's statements. He had their complete attention. "You have known me as Leader and only as Leader for far too long." Not a single citizen moved. You could almost say they were all in shock. "As of next first sun, I am stepping down as your Ruling Council's Leader and joining you as a common male." The shock went through the crowd as if the Ruling Council's Leader had told them to move would set off a bomb. They knew something terrible was coming, but not this. No Ruling Council's Leader had ever stepped down before. No one even knew the protocol for such a thing.

"As of first sun, I will be known as Streph, the name given me at my naming ceremony by my loving parents.

"Also, at first sun, my successor and all successors from all time hereafter will be known by the name given them at their ceremonies.

"The Ruling Council will be asking for you to decide who shall lead them.

"This will be done by your vote.

"As of first sun, Kladax will be known as an egalitarian planet.

"I thank you."

The citizens were silent. No one knew how to react to the news. It wasn't until the Ruling Council stepped down and started to walk amongst the crowd and stand with their families that anyone moved. Never before had the Ruling Council done such a thing and everyone asked their questions at the same time. Never had Kladax known their citizens to make such a noise before. Morgos found Grorth and they stood together with Anor and Travor, awaiting their turns with the citizens.

The mid point nutritional time found some of the citizens still unable to comprehend what had happened. The nutritional centres were crowded, as usual, but no one was ingesting. The nutritional platforms in the abodes were laden with items but no one was seated. Some abodes didn't even get so far as to prepare the nutrition. The citizens found they had something far more important than ingesting to occupy their thoughts but no one knew what to do.

It was during this time of confusion the Community Voice System came on and the voice of the newsreader started to explain what the announcements meant to them.

"At first sun," he told them, "the Ruling Council asks you to decide which amongst them you want to have lead them and us. You will be hearing from all of them at various times for the next seven suns and then you will cast your choice." He went on to tell everyone what voting was and where it would be held.

"It's all too much to think about, Morgos," Anor said. She was frightened and was unsure of what was happening to their lives. Streph was the only Ruling Council's Leader many of them had ever known. "Why do we have to have the changes all at once and so fast?" she asked.

"The Ruling Council decided as a group that it was time," he explained. "Just like the newsreader was saying, the Ruling Council felt, now that we have outworlders living amongst us, it was time to advance our society to welcome all forms of life and all beliefs. History tells us there have been many such planets and we can make this work if we take the best of all of them and then decide which is best for us."

Anor was still unsure of it all but she could see the sense of it. Kladax had been run by the Ruling Council since time immemorial and history also taught her that everything must end, even the best of things.

"But what if we make all of these changes to accommodate outworlders just to find out that there aren't any outworlders anymore? What if the Rnites accomplished what they set out to do and they found all of the cerium worth mining and in doing so killed every society out there? We would have changed, no killed, our own society for nothing." The tiny droplet on her cheek soon turned into a steady *clave* and Morgos held her close. He didn't know what to say so he said nothing but he was just as worried as she and maybe more so since he had spoken in favour of the changes.

Now he was wondering what he had done and how he could live with it if it all failed and his fellow citizens suffered because of it. He knew he needed someone else's ear to hear his concerns but who's. He couldn't go to any of the Ruling Council now that the deed was done. It would make him look weak and indecisive. He decided to approach Grorth. After all, Grorth and his crew were one of the major reasons these changes were to take place.

"I wish to have Grorth's opinion of what transpired this sun. I feel he and his crew should have a say in whether we change our society for them or if they should change to meet ours. I will voice him now and have him come to this abode as soon as he can."

Grorth was with his crew and they were discussing the gathering they had held some time before.

"I don't think we will need to make plans to leave now, Grorth. The citizens here seem to have accepted us well and we are settling in now. What do you think?" The crewman who spoke was usually the last one to be heard from and today was no exception. Grorth had asked for the others to be honest with him and they had. He knew they didn't really want to leave any more than he did, but the last thing he wanted was to be responsible for making any more citizens miserable just by being here. He knew they still had their enemies and some just wanted them to go. If they must, they could get their ship running in a very few rotations.

Grorth's right hand male, Smun, had told the others he wanted to stay but would do what the majority felt was right. He was enjoying having a say in what happened to him, but he didn't want to be selfish about it. He hadn't told them yet about Enu and he also knew the clock was ticking because of their promise to destroy the ship by the end of the next sun.

The three of them were still discussing the situation when the announcement bell rang. They looked at one another and no one was expecting guests. Simun rose and went to the entry to see Morgos standing there and he didn't' have his usual happy appearance about him that they had come to expect whenever he paid them a call.

"Enter, Morgos, and welcome."

Morgos went into the abode only far enough to allow Smun to close the entry and no further.

"Why do you not come in, Morgos?" Grorth asked.

Morgos was wishing at this point he had not come. But he had and they had bid him enter their abode so he knew he had to speak his mind with them. He took the seat offered him and started in on what was bothering him so very much.

"I am afraid we may have made a huge mistake and I needed to speak with you about it, if that is all right."

Relaxing and giving small laughs, the former Theasosians welcomed Morgos' thoughts.

"My betrothed told me she was afraid we may be making changes to our society to accommodate you and other travelers when there may not be any others out there." He related the complete story and then felt totally ashamed. He had made it sound as if these three were not worthy of the changes and that was not what he had meant at all.

Someone reached over and poured Morgos some of the last of the Theasos liquid so favoured by the crew. Morgos knew what an honour it was and how little they must have left. He thanked them for not being offended by his words.

"We would feel the same if our places were in the opposite," Grorth said. "We have been talking about the sun's events and it was an honour to us for your Ruling Council to do it, but we do not feel it was necessary. Change comes gradually, as I am sure you know, and I cannot speak for the others here but it is my belief what is bothering your lovely betrothed is that so many changes were made so quickly and were not allowed to come gradually and naturally. Would I be correct in these assumptions?"

"Yes, you are, and she is very fond of the Leader, as are so many others here, and his leaving the Ruling Council is quite a blow to us. By tradition, the Ruling Council's Leader is in that role for life and to have one retire is unheard of, not only in our life periods, but ever."

"Is his retirement because it is something he feels he should do, or for other reasons?" Grorth asked. Then he had second thoughts about asking. "I apologize, Morgos. I have asked something that is not of my business and is very likely a personal decision. Please forgive me."

"No, that is quite all right, Grorth. It really isn't any secret. I have been on the Ruling Council for the better part of my mature rotations and the Leader has been talking about stepping down for almost all of those rotations. I have thought for the last three or four of those that he might actually do it and he has.

"I was sitting in the Ruling Council gathering when he made the suggestions we change to adapt to outworlders coming to live here and then in the very next breath he announced his plans to step down. We had just finished voicing our choices and were primed for a discussion on the results, in case of a tie or in case an uncommitted voice, and he presented us with his news.

"I had been nervous about the anticipated discussion because I knew in my heart I had gone the incorrect way and that would have been my opportunity to change my voice without disgrace or embarrassment. Now it is done and I have to find a way of voicing my dissention without loosing my hard earned respect as a Council member." He stopped for thought and the others respectfully waited. It was obvious that there was more to come and they were most interested in what he had to suggest, thus giving the reason for his visit.

"I do not mean to be blunt, but do you know if they received any answer at all to their attempt to reach Rnos?"

Grorth and his crew shook their heads sadly.

"I am sorry, Morgos, but they did not say and we did not ask. Their emotions were black when they returned to the surface."

"I understand. I will have to ask them directly, which is something I was going to do anyway. It was just my hope not to have to involve them at such a low period of their lives.

"It is my hope to put all of this behind us if we can prove there isn't anyone else out there. I know how painful this is for you to hear, and I am sorry, but I must face my thoughts and it is quite possible I will be proven correct." Morgos was feeling even worse now than when he arrived. All he wanted was for all of this to be over and done with, one way or the other, and then he could get on with his miserable life.

Morgos took his leave and slowly made his way to the visitors' abode. He really didn't want to put the idea to them while their spirits were low, but he wanted to get it over with and sometimes, he found, if you were already down, hearing more bad news was easier to handle. However, he also knew it could put them so low they may never recover. Facing the possibility they were all alone could not be easy at any time, but to have someone else confirm your fears could be worse than anything you could do to yourself. He had to admire Grorth and his men for the way they had faced this same dilemma.

Morgos wasn't quite sure how he was going to approach the subject he had arrived at the Rnite's abode and the one called Codid had seen him arrive. Morgos took a deep breath and greeted Codid as he was shown in.

"Greetings," the one called Znow said. "What brings you here this sun?" The way of the Rnite, Morgos was finding, was direct and to the point and he usually would be affronted by it but at this visit he was happy. It meant he wouldn't have time to fumble with his speech.

"We, the Ruling Council, are saddened by your failure to raise your people. How may we help?" Not the best, but it would have to do.

"We appreciate your thoughts," said Znow, "but there is not much that can be done. We realized when we failed to raise the support ship and all we received from Rnos was static that there wasn't anyone out there at all.

"We have been doing the private grief ritual and had just finished when you arrived."

"Please excuse my interruption. I shall go and we can talk when the time is better. I should have realized you would have a private ceremony, also."

"Why?"

"Pardon?"

"Why should you know anything about our rituals and customs?" He wasn't being nasty when he asked, but genuinely curious.

"It only makes sense that you would wish to say goodbye to your fellow Rnites using your own customs. Even though we are having an official day of mourning at the new sun, a private time together makes sense. After all, we are just learning about each other's customs, aren't we?"

The Rnites looked at Morgos and didn't move or even blink. They were making him feel most uncomfortable but he refused to babble like the idiot he felt he was. He just kept looking back at them until finally the one called Datron spoke.

"This is ridiculous. We are not going home and these people have shown us nothing but kindness and consideration since we got here. Why are we acting like we would if we were on Rnos? Morgos knows us better than that. Certainly, he knows we grieve but that does not mean we have to be uncivil, does it? Morgos, you are always welcome here at our abode."

"Thank you, Datron. You also at mine. Now, to get to why I really came. I was at the Ruling Council gathering when the new changes were announced and voiced on and even thought I voiced in favour at the time, I now cannot support my voice. I need to know how you feel about there being the possibility of anyone else out there so I can call a discussion and change my support."

The three visitors all spoke at once but Morgos could tell they were all saying the same thing, just in different ways. There was no one left out there within voice range to contact and the changes were the first step in another unified world.

He stayed a decent amount of time and then took his leave, making sure they understood they were welcome at his abode at any time and to visit him at the office whenever they wished.

"I would also like to do one more thing before I leave you," he said.

"Yes, Morgos?" Znow queried.

"From here on out it would please me to cease calling you 'the visitors' and address you by the names given you at birth. To me, you are now, and have been for some time, members of this community and I wish to treat you as such."

"We are honoured, Morgos." The three newest members of the society gave a respectful bow and saw their guest to the entry. Little did Morgos realize how pleased they really were by his actions.

Morgos returned to his abode and he was tired, but he felt he had done what he had to do and all had turned out well. He would ask the Ruling Council for a discussion after the ceremonies at the rising sun. He quietly crept into the sleeping area he shared with Anor and slid slowly onto the platform. He was too tired to undress and he knew Anor would chastise him for it when he woke, but for the moment he really did not care. He was asleep before he had time to even remove his foot apparel.

First Period of Change

The first rays of sun found fewer members of the community at the Rnite ceremony for the dead but those that were there called themselves friends to the three surviving Rnites. Those that had thoughts of going with negative feelings were asked to stay away and respect the fact that the visitors had gone to their ceremony with respect for their dead. It would only be polite to reciprocate those feelings at the Rnite ceremony. To go anywhere with negative thoughts towards those being honoured was considered worse than rude anyway and for that reason alone no one should have even had thoughts along that path. But curiosity would draw some to the raised platform and as long as they were polite they would go virtually unnoticed. But just in case, the Ruling Council had people walking through the crowd to make sure. It was another first for Kladax and just one more thing the Ruling Council was most uncomfortable with, mainly because they didn't know where the change of attitude had come from and it frightened them more than just a bit. Some on the Ruling Council were counting the days until their terms of officer ended and they could hand these problems on to someone else.

The visitors mounted the raised platform and waited for quiet, which came quickly. Codid stepped forward and spoke to those assembled.

"I will be explaining what is happening as we go along and then when the ceremony is complete, the three of us would be most pleased to answer any questions you may have. We begin." He stepped back and the three of them began a haunting chant.

No stories were told and no songs were sung, just chants, and it still left many who watched in tears. When the ceremony was completed, the three visitors then left the raised platform and walked amongst those few who had stayed, smiling and thanking them for being there. As they started t leave, the Ruling Council's former Leader, now known as Streph, stood on the raised platform and called for silence.

"I am no longer your Ruling Council's Leader, but as my last act as such I have an announcement." No one spoke or moved. They did not know what Streph could have to say.

"At the last gathering of the Ruling Council, it was decided that we have been calling those from Rnite 'visitors' long enough. Therefore, as of this sun they will be known as, and called, Kladaxions.

"It has taken us far too long to also offer the same to those from Theasos. We have joined them in our hearts and minds but have not made them ours by name. So, welcome to all of the new Kladaxions.

"Finally, let this period be called the First Period of Enlightenment. We are fast approaching our rainy season, so let us see it as a cleansing not only of the soil but of our souls and face the future as a whole people." He removed his Robes of Office and handed them to the member of council closest to him. He then left the raised platform and walked amongst his people, bowing and smiling at each and every one. To look upon his face was to see contentment and peace. The people could see he had made the right decision.

Morgos, Anor with little Travor by the hand, Grorth and his crew and the former Rnites all came together and Morgos very formally bowed to the newest citizens of Kladax.

"This is a good revolution, my friends," he said, "and we must celebrate together."

Smun cleared his throat in such a way his friends, new and old, knew he had something of importance to say. They waited politely for him to find his voice, which he very seldom lost, and that brought smirks to his fellow crewmen's faces.

"I thank you," he began as equally formally as Morgos had before him, "but I must confess that no celebration of our acceptance here on Kladax would be complete if I were not to share another happiness in my heart." The rest of the former Theasosians gasped. They knew only too well the formal words and knew what was coming. They were about to have their fondest wish put into words and spoken into the air.

"I would be most grateful," Smun continued, "if the celebration we are about to undertake could also be shared by the one who has stolen my heart."

He got no further. Grorth and his men picked him up and tossed him into the air, shouting their pleasures at the top of their lungs. The few who remained from the previous celebrations watched in amazement and joy. Never before had they seen such a demonstration.

"Enu!" Grorth called out. "Enu! Come out of hiding, you darling, wonderful thing you!"

From out of the crowd came Enu, a pretty little thing with eyes that were not only the deepest of purple but eyes that allowed one to see right into her soul, which was as pure and as innocent as they come.

Grorth walked slowly up to the shy girl in place of Smun's male parent and reached for her hands, which he surrounded with his huge ones.

"I have been at two or three announcements of bonding while we have been here, Enu, and each one has pleased me to no end. But the fact that our shy, withdrawn Smun has found and declared love with and for you pleases me the most." He waited patiently while the cheering from the crowd went on and on. When it finally died down, he continued. "It is, I mean, was the custom of Theasos that the female adult declared their bonding day. Here on our new home of Kladax, it is the male who declares. So it shall be your bonding, I am sure, Enu. But do not let him wait too long. For he is of the disposition that, if given the chance, he will never properly bond and he will run for the hills like a *schlink*!"

"Oh, no he won't!" Enu declared. This brought the expected and traditional laughter and then Grorth became serious once again.

"Please do us the honour of being our guest at a most joyous double celebration of acceptance and of bonding. You and Smun will hold the seats of honour, with your parents at your side, we hope."

"They will be there, as will I." The cheering was so loud Enu could not hear herself tell Smun that she loved him. He could not hear himself tell her that his love for her held no bounds. Their eyes told each other they could hardly wait to be alone.

Word had reached the finest nutritional centres in the community and all were prepared for the onslaught of celebrants to arrive. Each one would have been honoured to host such a double celebration and the proprietors pulled out their delicacies and house specialities. But each was to be disappointed, for the expected crowd never arrived at any of these fine establishments, for they never got the chance to leave the square.

People from all over the community, when hearing of the upcoming betrothal of one of their favourite children, swarmed over the happy couple and their friends and presented them with a feast fit for a Ruling Council founding member. They ran and acquired nutritional platforms, items to place upon them, seats, liquids and more celebrants. The party went on for revolutions.

None of the newest members of the community felt slighted that their acceptance celebration had been taken over by the bonding celebration because that was what had made them the happiest. By the time Grorth and the rest of the merry makers found their way back to their abodes, not one of them would say it wasn't just the best celebration they had ever attended.

Late that darkness, Grorth and two of his crew quietly went up in their tiny ship.

The revolutions following the end of the conflict time and celebrations that were held after were busy ones for the community. There were many preparations to be made before the nua arrived and the walkways flooded and many new laws to learn, but the most important was the new Ruling Council and the final changes they had made to the governing of Kladax. The people would have a say in the laws of the community and the way in which those who chose to break them were punished. It had been many hundreds of revolutions since such laws were needed and the Ruling Council was in agreement that it most likely would be many hundreds more before they were needed once again, but because of recent activity, the

Ruling Council felt these laws should be there, so they were entered into the Book of Laws and became official.

But the law that no one knew how to deal with was the Law of Votes. Until then, only the Ruling Council voted the new members in and then amongst themselves voted to pass motions and other necessary items of business. But hence forward, the people of Kladax would be voting for their future Ruling Council, its Leader and all major laws. The Ruling Council had set up a series of information gatherings for the citizens to be properly indoctrinated into the process and the general population was quite sceptical about it all but by the second gathering they were getting accustomed to the new way of thinking. Having a say in which direction their community would go was starting to sound quite exciting.

Grorth had attended the gatherings where the citizens were introduced to the last of the proposed changes and those who wished to have their names put forward for the Ruling Council, the Ruling Council's Leader and was honoured to be considered eligible for the vote. Morgos, just by the fact that he held a seat on the Ruling Council, was eligible for the election but held no hope of even being nominated for the Ruling Council's Leader. The seat he held was of a minor one and still had many revolutions to serve before he could be seriously considered. He therefore threw his support behind the one member he felt would make the best Ruling Council's Leader, Cloa, and attended all of the gatherings held to get Cloa's views out to the public. Besides, he may not even have a seat after the vote, Morgos thought, and at least his feelings and wishes would be represented on the Ruling Council when Cloa took his seat.

The rotation of the vote came quickly; too quickly for some. Many were almost afraid to go to put their marks for their candidates, still thinking this all to be a bad joke and when they arrived they would be told no. But, go they did, and in tremendous numbers.

By the time Morgos and Anor arrived, they found themselves at the back of a line that went around the building and then some. Neither had seen so many people gathered in one place since the gathering. When their turn finally came, it had been dark for some time.

"It's almost like we are shlums being led to slaughter," Anor said as they gained entrance to the building.

"What do you mean?"

"Well, think about it for a while. This is the first time any of us has ever done anything like this and what do we really know about it? We are going to vote and we are still very much in the dark as to where all of this will lead us.

"We just have to have faith that we mark for the right person, and we won't know until he takes his seat and starts representing us if we have done the right thing.

"What if we haven't? Then where will that leave us? Can we ask him to leave, or will it take another vote? I don't' know. Do you?"

Morgos could hear the tears in his betrothed's voice and the fear she had was written on her face and in her eyes. He hated to see her this way and he knew he had to calm her fear quickly or she would alert some of the others around them and then the fear would spread like the wild fires their planet had suffered from eons ago, destroying their friends as their last remaining trees had been destroyed. This voting was new to everyone and it would only work if everyone had faith that it would. All it would take to destroy it forever was one person, Anor, sending her tremendous fear into the hearts of others.

Trying to keep the trembling from his voice, he gently placed his hands on his betrothed's shoulders, looked into her eyes and reminded her of the third public gathering, held not five rotations before.

"Remember when the Ruling Council told us they had put it into place that if an elected one did not fulfill his duties, or if those who elected him felt he wasn't working hard enough, he could be replaced?"

"I remember." Anor was starting to once again feel the excitement of her friends and neighbours, but she wasn't totally convinced what they were doing was right. Something kept telling her there had to be a better way. But what? She had no idea. "I remember what they told us, all right, but did they tell us fact? Or just what they thought would make us feel good about this voting thing?"

"Please be calm, my betrothed. It will be all right. Maybe not all of those who win a seat are the beat ones to be there, but only time will tell us that. Besides, according to the new law, we can go back and vote again in two revolutions. Not that long, really, when you stop to think about it."

Searching her betrothed's eyes, she felt better, somewhat, and thanked him for his help. Maybe she was just overreacting, she thought to herself. Something she was want to do whenever anything new came into her life that she didn't completely understand, or trust. She decided to carry through with her voting and maybe, at least, put her betrothed's mind at ease, if not her own.

"Maybe it is because I am still a bit frightened of this whole voting thing and all of the new laws. It has been too sudden for me."

Morgos hugged her tightly and led her inside after handing someone standing at the door and their right to vote papers had been checked and stamped. They then accepted the list of those they could choose from and entered the little areas cordoned off for each person. Morgos was quick to make his marks and was standing by Anor's area, waiting for her, as she struggled. Morgos knew his betrothed had appeared to be happier about voting, but he knew she had done it for him. It was going to be a long wait for the results but Morgos was willing to have a smile on his face the whole time, if only to show Anor how successful, and pleasant, the process could be. He just hoped he was right.

Meanwhile, Anor, closed in her tiny space and with the names before her, was on the verge of total collapse. What if she did the wrong thing and her community had to pay for her mistakes? But could just one vote do that, she wondered. Could one little vote put the whole community in danger like that? Those that sat through the first gathering had been told over and over again that every vote mattered, that every vote counted. She had to do the right thing, if for no other reason than to give her homeland a good start on their new life.

Anor was about to walk out, turn her back on her first opportunity to help change their world, when it came to her like a bolt of lightening. Her one little vote, her one lone voice, couldn't possibly do all that damage to her friends and family. There were thousands of single votes and one wasn't going to make all that much difference, if any at all, in the long and short of things.

She then bent over the small platform, took writing tool in hand, and made her strokes, strong and true. As she left the enclosure, she felt good about partaking in the process and knew that this new thing called open politics was for everyone, not just those in power. She also knew, silly as it sounded, that even if the wrong person was put into power, it would take more than her vote to put him there, and it would take more than her vote to remove him. She was just a tiny little piece in this huge machine, but she was one of the tiny little pieces that helped make it go. Her thoughts were making her feel rather childish and foolish, so she put her head up straight, back tight and joined her betrothed, trying to portray a confidence she still didn't totally feel, but was much better than when she had left Morgos to make his marks.

She found Morgos waiting for her with a smile on his face that, when she looked at him again, wasn't quite right.

"Ready?"

She smiled back at him, dropped her list into the container after his and they put their arms around each other and as they headed for the entrance. That was when Anor realized by the tightness of his back muscles Morgos was just as nervous as she had been, but he had managed to hide it better than she had and she loved him even more for it.

They slowly made their way home to await the final count and to see who had won permanent five revolution seats on the new Ruling Council.

The new Vote Count committee wanted to insure perfection and this required them to take the rest of the darkness period and almost the entire sun to count all of the marks and make the announcement, declaring the winners. They had, sometime during the darkness time, to start over because of a conflict in a count and there must be no conflict or mismatch in anything. The rules were explicit and the committee was, and wanted, to follow the rules to the letter, thus, not a word was spoken by anyone other than those required to communicate the names and their numbers from then out. By the time of the pre-sun, they had created a flowing system, and almost a third of the votes counted, making the process go very quickly. None of the committee was to know how hard their jobs were going to be when they had signed up for this, but not one of them wanted to leave, either. Many of them would end up going around the sun, and then some, without benefit of rest or companionship of their loved ones.

"I hope," said the third level counter, "that the next vote is more organized than this" when the last of the marks were being written on the first page of the Vote Registry. They had chosen the fifth level counter to do this great honour as his marks were always the neatest and most awed over and they wanted the future generations to be able to appreciate this darkness and sun and what it had meant to those who were there.

"Meaning?" the fifth level asked, without taking his eyes off, or slowing down on, his entry work. The two levels had been arguing with everything the other had said since before the New Laws were announced, and the other counters couldn't help but ask themselves why this time should be any different. It was most difficult to ascertain that the two had once been related by betrothal of their mutual female siblings.

"Meaning," the third level said with more than a little sharpness to his tongue, "that we signed on for this position not knowing that we would have to count not just our community, but all of the others that also had residents making their marks. I had just assumed that each community would be doing their own counting, that is all I meant." He glared at his former relative. "Had you given this any thought at all?" Then he did the almost unforgiveable. Smiling, he then added, "I am so sorry, former sibling-in-law. I had quite forgotten. You are not capable of independent thought away from she who gave birth to you, are you?"

He knew the moment the words left his mouth he had gone too far and had violated every decency law their planet had ever had; but he also knew he could not take those hateful, hurtful words back. Once spoken, always heard was the current saying, and he knew he would have to pay the penalty for them. What made it all the worse was he knew his words to be true, but also a family secret shared with no one, and were part of a much larger story that would never be told, and it certainly wasn't his fault it was his betrothed that had died instead of the other. Grief was making him do some really stupid things, especially to those he was supposed to support and care for. He had turned what started out to be an innocent thought and feeling into an inexcusable insult to a person he once loved and admired.

He also knew his days of serving his fellow community members were over. Without saying a word, he rose from his seat and walked toward the entrance. No one looked at him, no one said a word of comfort, and he listened for none, as he knew he did not deserve them. He would face the New Ruling Council at the next sun and then bid his world good-bye. His only hope now was that the Ruling Council would allow him to die at his own hand as a symbolic gesture of apology to one and all. But he doubted it very much, for that right was strictly reserved for those who had served well and with honour, something he had never done, especially this sun. As he walked away, he wondered if it were possible to miss those he loved in life while dwelling in the afterlife.

He was about to find out.

The new Vote Counter committee announced the winners of the vote immediately after meeting with the Ruling Council at the next sun and it was decreed there would be no more mention of what was now being called 'the incident', either amongst themselves or out in public as per order of the Ruling Council. It would be their last, and least liked, secret order and a memory they would all like, but be unable, to forget. Ever. The community members would wonder for some time whatever happened to that fellow, and then more pressing matters would take over their thought processes. The subject was closed before it even had a chance to open.

When the list of winners was read out, the winners' supporters cheered loudly and waved their support articles in the air, feeling good about voting. When those who had voted for another heard they had lost, many of them declared loudly that everyone should watch for their candidates at the next vote, and that brought even louder cheering. There didn't' seem to be any sorrowful feelings, only happiness about their participation in an historical event.

It came as quite a surprise to Morgos, then, when his candidate was not voted back in but he was, and due to the number of votes he had received, as First Assistant to the Ruling Council's Leader. His candidate was the first to congratulate him shortly after and found, like the former Ruling Council's Leader, Streph, retirement was in his future.

So, using these two fine law regulators as examples, the Ruling Council's last law to be voted into being was one of retirement. It stated that no elected Ruling Council member could serve beyond the biological rotation of ninety without special permission of the Ruling Council. That would leave the citizen's servant many rotations to enjoy without the shackles of government holding him down.

But the most exciting celebration of these passing rotations of long standing tradition was the bonding of Smun and Enu.

There wasn't a citizen missing and not a nau eye in the square as they shared their devotion to each other and promised their families support in their elder rotations, even though Smun's promise went to Enu's parents instead of his. He had taken them on as his own, as had they he and it brought great pride to his heart.

When they made their promises to raise their children in the traditional manner, the newly betrothed looked down at the child who reclined in the special seat between them and smiled broadly. Their female child looked up at them and wondered what it was all about, but at only five portions of a rotation, she was too young to understand, or appreciate, what this revolution meant.

Not only was she a child of love but a child of the future. The proud parents really didn't care what their child was called but in love they had started calling her a Kladaos and it seemed to satisfy her, not that she knew what they were talking about. Because none of the other betrothed couples from Theasos and Kladax had been able to bear children, this child was even more of a miracle and gave the others hope that they may still have families of their own.

Enu and Smun had also decided to break with Kladax and Theasos traditions and have the naming ceremony when the child they shared saw her first full revolution instead of the first appearance of her maturity horn and that was held the rotation after her parents' bonding ceremony. More residents of the community, and others, attended the ceremony than had attended the day before, if that were at all possible.

The ceremony began, as tradition prescribed, at first sun and the parents were more excited about this than they were their bonding. They arrived at the raised platform in the square well ahead of any of their family or friends and there were still people from the community ahead of them. At the appointed portion of the rotation, the two proud parents mounted the raised platform with their child, riding in a chair made by their linked arms, and the crowd instantly settled down. No one wanted to miss this long awaited moment.

"Thank you for coming to our child's naming ceremony," Smun said. "My betrothed and I searched long and hard for the correct name for our girl child. We wanted a name that would reflect both her Theasos and her Kladax heritages and yet be a name all her own."

"We also wanted her name to reflect that she is the first of a new species of being and we wanted her to have pride in being such. We searched all the old texts from as many worlds as we could and we found what we feel is a most unique name. It comes from Earth's old Sanskrit language and means New Creation.

"Therefore," Enu said, as she looked first at her child and then her betrothed, "we have decided on the name Navaracanaa and will be known as Nava. What could be more fitting for the first child of a new species, and a new nationality?" Looking down at the now totally confused child, Enu said "Welcome, little Nava, to the new and truly blended Kladax."

The crowd went absolutely wild and the cries from the startled child could not be heard by even her parents, who held her in their arms. The laughter from the adults confused and startled her even more, and her cries even louder. It was time to remove the child to the safety, and quiet, of her own home and her bed. As the small family was leaving the platform, the first drops of the desperately needed, and gratefully early, nua fell. Anor and Smun looked to the skies and thanked Olag, for it had been an especially hard nau this rotation and many were without enough liquid to see themselves through many more revolutions. Even those who had been sharing had had to say no lately and it was most difficult to do so.

Many of the crowd rushed to their abodes to finish the preparations that they had put aside for the betrothal and naming ceremonies. Because the nua had started early, many had put off even beginning their preparations and had been caught without anything done, and they ran the fastest. If they did not finish before the nua reached its hardest, many would find the liquid go into the planet's surface and they would find themselves without enough in their storage devices to last the nau.

Enu and Smun had taken care to have their preparations finished at the time of their betrothal so they could focus on the last two rotations. They knew, however, than many in the community were not ready so they left the child with Enu's female parent and they rushed off to help those most in need. They knew they had a very short period of time and all energies would have to be put toward helping others. Grorth and many more of his crewmen, along with Morgos, the old and the new Ruling Councils and many more, were already hard at work.

The complete community worked the rotation around and well into the next. The nua not only came early but heavy almost immediately. The citizens only had portions of a rotation's warning the nua were going to get heavy so Grorth, with the help of those that weren't busy on other duties, repaired and prepared the community storage device. This device was the most important, as the community relied on it for back up liquid during the worst of the coming nau. Without it, vast numbers would be without liquid for many rotations. It never mattered how well one prepared, there was always a call for the extra liquid, and this revolution would be no different.

The nua came and kept coming for seventeen rotations. Abodes were safe because of the tradition of building them high and on slopes, but many nutritional animals and abode pets were lost. On the fifth rotation, the fresh and saline liquids mixed and contaminated much of the planet's surface. On the tenth rotation, the remaining nutritional animals drown. On the fourteenth rotation, everything below the level of the abodes was under liquid. On the seventeenth rotation, the nua slowed and by the forty-first rotation had ceased and the intense heat returned.

It took the citizens another forty-five rotations to clean up the damage and account for all of the dead animals. By then, the heat had stabilized and another nua season was over. The liquid storage device held, to a certain extent, and those who were not able to finish their preparations had liquid. For those that did, the device allowed them to leave what it contained for those who did not.

All of the citizens were grateful, once again, for the mandatory animal registration. It made the search for them so easy and efficient because of the location discs they wore. Many citizens complained about the registration being mandatory for each and every animal in the community, with no exceptions, when it was first introduced because they saw it as just another governmental control, but after the next nua season, they were applauding the foresight of the Ruling Council. They had all animals accounted for in less than five rotations, where in nua past, it had taken as long as a full revolution to accomplish the task.

When the new Ruling Council's Leader called Grorth after the clean up had been accomplished to appear before them, he voiced Morgos to see if he would provide him with some insight as to what the Ruling Council required of him. All Morgos could tell him was, as far as Morgos was concerned, Grorth would be pleased.

Grorth attended the Ruling Council's gathering with a great deal of apprehension but also some pride in the work he had done for his new community. He knew the old Ruling Council had a habit of taking a small item and turning it into a three rotation event. He was still becoming accustomed to receiving, and accepting, praise for his work and because of his comfort level, or lack of it, he hope the new Ruling Council didn't follow the old Ruling Council and make a large showing of such a little thing as a storage device for liquid.

He arrived at the Ruling Council's chambers and waited to be asked to enter. When he was shown in and given a seat, he then waited for the Ruling Council's Leader to speak. When he did, Grorth was astounded.

"Grorth, we, the Ruling Council, asked you here today to not only commend you on your work during the nua season but also for your help in rebuilding the top floor of the building damaged during the attack of the Rnites.

"Your plans for the cleanup and rebuilding were of tremendous aide and the assistance you and your crew provided during the rush the nua caused cannot be cast aside. Because of this, this Ruling Council wished to designate the chair you are now sitting occupying as yours." The Ruling Council's Leader looked Grorth straight in the eyes, lowered his voice and then said, "Please say you will accept this honour, Grorth. Presenting you with medals, honours and the like is just for the pleasure of the public and are soon forgotten. By asking you to accept this seat on the Ruling Council, with full benefits and entitlements, we are asking for your continued input into the operations, both daily and continually, of this community and to tell you how grateful we have been for your assistance to date.

"As you may be aware, this award has never been done before, and none of us," he said, looking at the rest of the Ruling Council, both for confirmation and for support, "really know if it is even legal. But we all agreed that we must go over and above anything that had been done in the past because you, and your crew, have done what has never been done before, and we truly don't know how to reward something like this.

"You and your men have embraced this planet as your own, as have we, and you have all gone far further than any of us had ever expected when you declared your acceptance of us as your new people.

"We wish we could award all of you this seat, but, of course, that is impossible. So, we ask that you accept on the behalf of you and your crew and sit on this Ruling Council, not only to represent your own, but the community, which are also your own, now.

The Ruling Council's Leader was looking quite uncomfortable and had started to pace in place and seemed he didn't quite know where to place his hands. Grorth knew he had to rescue the poor man, and quickly, before it got any worse and went from just discomfort to total embarrassment for all of them. This showing of the emotions of the Ruling Council's Leader, and the Ruling Council itself, was unheard of and considered very rude.

Grorth's own upbringing and personal code of ethics prevented him from feeling pride but he couldn't help it. He had arrived at the gathering with every intent of not letting whatever they had to say to him to interfere with those ethics but he just couldn't do it. He never expected their thank you's to go beyond the words and here they were offering him a seat on the Ruling Council. But his first concern had to be the Ruling Council's Leader and with that, Grorth found it easier to focus his mind away from his own conflicts.

"Ruling Council, Leader. I thank you for this tremendous honour. When we sought this planet out, it was out of desperation to escape a deadly enemy and to land before we ran out of fuel." Grorth stopped for a moment, thinking back to those days, and the pain they had caused every aboard his tiny ship, and then he brought himself back to the present. Taking a deep breath to help compose himself, he continued. "None of us ever expected to be welcomed as you have and we will never be able to thank you for what you have done for us. Now, here you are, after we tried to help and to do our best doing it to pay a little of that kindness back, you are offering us not only a permanent home but a chance to have a say in the way in which our home is run. I accept this seat, not for myself, but for my crew and the future generations of the new species to follow. May they realize their coming to be is because two different species learned to live, work and love together, in harmony and mutual respect."

Grorth left the Ruling Council chambers not knowing exactly how he was feeling. Had this entire episode taken place on Theasos he would not even have been singled and life would not have changed for him. He would have known he had done what had needed to be done and that would have been the end of it. The Ruling Council had brought forth emotions, and feelings, Grorth had never felt before and they almost scared him. He needed time to absorb everything that had happened to him in a relatively short span of time.

He arrived back at his abode and was greeted on the welcoming path by Enu and several more of the ladies of the community. They were carrying nutritional items and various liquids. He rushed to open his entry and allow them into his abode.

"What is all of this?"

"What does it look like, Grorth?" Enu asked, pretending not to understand his confusion. She allowed him a few moments and then gave him a serious look.

"Morgos informed me last dark period that you were going to be offered a seat at the Ruling Council table and he fully expected you to accept." She laughed when she saw his shocked look. "He told me how they had worked it all out," she continued, "and he tried to think of everything you would use to decline, and how they could counter attack them." She leaned over to him and gently kissed his cheek. That was something else she had picked up from her reading books from other planets. It felt strange to him, but in a way he rather liked it. "The Ruling Council was going to make sure you accepted their honour, one way or another," she went on, "but they also wanted to be sure you did so when you were ready. We are all so pleased you were ready this sun."

When Grorth was finally able to regain his senses, he gazed at the other female adults in his abode and realized they were all betrothed's to other Ruling Council members. It was a conspiracy and he had no way out. He started laughing and couldn't stop, until he heard his announcement bell ringing.

Still chuckling, he went to the entry and wasn't at all surprised the other members of the Ruling Council, including the Leader, were standing there, along with the rest of his crew members.

"Enter," invited and stepped to on side. By the time everyone was in, there wasn't anywhere he could go. The abode was packed with friends and neighbours and the noise was tremendous. It was at that point someone suggested they move to the raised platform in the community square and give everyone a chance to stretch and move around. Smelling another set-up, Grorth laughed and went along with the crowd. As he expected, the rest of the community was there, waiting for him. Grorth had never felt such love and acceptance and he was suddenly quite overwhelmed. But the pressing crowd didn't give him much time to dwell on it. The partiers had already got a head start and he was determined to enjoy every bit of it.

Sometime during the festivities, Grorth's eye caught sight of a lady he had not met, and he thought he knew all of the ladies of the community. Thinking her to be new, he wandered over and tried to introduce himself.

"Yes," she said, not allowing him to speak. "I know who you are. My name is Maeho and I am the daughter of the vom of the omn of Morgos and I have just returned from the other side of the landmass. Anor has told me all about you and your experiences and I must say I am very impressed."

Astounded, he asked "Impressed? Why? What is there to be impressed about with me?" Grorth was quickly becoming shy and more than a little embarrassed. To think, someone was impressed with him, for whatever reason. He wanted to hear more, yet didn't. He didn't want to encourage this beautiful female, but he did hope she would explain herself. In detail. He was starting to feel the tug of guilt, because on Theasos to feel pleasure from a compliment was considered extremely rude and beyond the acceptable level of personal ego. He had been trained from early childhood to graciously acknowledge the accolade but to feel nothing personally, and here he was, practically dancing, waiting to hear more from this lovely being by his side. What was wrong with him? He had never felt like this before, and he hoped the feeling never left him. But worst of all, he hoped none of his crew could see him now. He knew he wasn't hiding his feelings very well and now wasn't the time to have his crew loose faith in him. He shook his head slowly, and imperceptivity, he hoped. He turned his eyes to look Maeho straight into her eyes and listened closely.

"I am impressed that you and your men would go out of your way to help virtual strangers, that's all." Maeho returned his gentle stare. "You must have been thinking you would eventually move on and therefore there wasn't any kind of commitment to our planet or its people. Am I right, or am I right?" She couldn't hide her amusement at her words and they shared a laugh. He loved her laugh. It reminded him, only slightly, of his wife's. No, he wasn't going there. He wasn't going to get sad. Not right now, anyway. He would pay homage to her later, in the privacy of his abode, where no one could see, or hear, him. He still hadn't been able to let go. Not completely. But that was his other life. This was now, and he truly wanted to be in the here and now, even if leaving the past behind was so hard. He returned his attention to the beautiful Maeho. Then he found himself right where she wanted him – speechless – and she had done it with nothing other than the truth. What was her game, he thought. What ever it was, he found he was more than willing to play.

"You are correct, Naeho. My crew and I had, at one point, made plans to leave Kladax but then we not only realized there wasn't anywhere for us to go, but we actually liked living here and we had fallen in love with the people. Some of us more than the rest, as you probably have heard."

Naeho was pleased to hear of Grorth's acceptance of his and his crew's fate from Grorth himself. It told her it wasn't just idle or wishful gossip, but the truth. They had put their previous lives behind them, as much as they could, and had embraced life on Kladax to the fullest, or as close to the fullest as they could at the present time. Her heart went out to them, in one way, because they had lost everything, but in another way, she couldn't have been happier. They had barely met and here she was, thinking thoughts that would have been considered in bad taste if anyone else could have heard them. She blushed slightly and then turned with her full attention on what he was doing and saying. It was as if he was the only other person there and it was a feeling she had never quite experienced before. But she liked it. A lot.

They shared a small laugh over an even smaller joke and Grorth walked her to the liquid platform. Pouring each of them a holder of the first thing his hand came to, because he really couldn't take his eyes off her, he looked down just in time to see he had a holder of one of the many different types of nutritional protein toppers.

"That does it!" he shouted. "Now I have gone and made a total *threp* of myself." Before he could take another breath, he heard his star navigator shout at him and to the crowd in general.

"Grorth has finally fallen in love!"

He couldn't say a word, because he had. From the top of his crown to his wide webbed feet, he was in love and he didn't care who knew. He knew it didn't make any sense. They hadn't even known each other a full rotation and here he was, getting ready to ask her to bond with him. It was totally, completely crazy.

"What would you say," he started.

"When would you like the bonding ceremony?"

That was it! She even knew what he was gong to say before he said it, and at times before he himself knew what it was he wanted to say. He felt like an adolescent once more. He didn't know what to say, where to put his hands and he couldn't keep his feet still. All he could do was to gently take her hand in his and grin. But what pleased him the most was she felt the same way.

"Better get bonded as quickly as possible, Grorth! That's the only way you'll be of any use to anyone ever again." Morgos was standing next to him and he hadn't even seen or heard him come close.

Grorth and Naeho spent their dark period away from the rest of the ceremony by taking a long walk in the moonlight from the three moons and feeling the soft moss under their feet. They took in the fragrance of the flowers and they sweet darkness breeze. If someone had said to Grorth just a rotation earlier he would feel this way and enjoy being with another person this much he would have called them crazy. Now, he was the one that was crazy. Crazy in love. The only thing missing was being able to share all of this with his male co-offspring. Their parents died when they were both very young so they were all each other had and they shared everything. Grorth was at his male co-olffspring's bonding and he abided the teasing his friends and his male co-offspring about how it would, one rotation, be his turn for bonding and he would be the first to tell him to start a new life. Grorth also knew his betrothed would understand and not stand in his way. All they had wanted for each other was happiness, and Grorth knew he would have given her his blessings had she been the one to be standing here and he had been the one to fall to the Rnites.

The walk came to an end far too quickly and Grorth was totally useless the next sun. How happy could one person be?

The bonding ceremony was held during the Seasons of the Flowers when the parched soil puts forth a carpet of brilliant reds and blues for a few short rotations and then they are gone, to be followed by stark and barren soil.

Naeho had chosen bonding robes with a blend of the colours of the flowers and her head was festooned with the blooms freshly plucked from the fields. She presented her beloved a bouquet of the same as a symbol of her love, beautiful and soft, and he her to symbolize his renewing love for her. With each consecutive Season of Flowers, the colours would seem brighter and fresher than the season before and that was how he wanted his love for her to be, brighter and bolder than the season before. Everyone at the ceremony commented they had never seen the blooms so bright or so fragrant.

The Nau

The nau was the longest in recent memory and it took its toll on both the land and the people. In past revolutions, if an abode or the liquid storage devices hadn't, for whatever reason, managed to collect enough liquid, the inhabitants of the abode would suffer thirst and some would go to meet Olag before their time. It was always a struggle to stay alive during this period and there were many rotations where families had had to scrape to find enough liquid to get through the last few rotations before the nua came once again because they did not have their own devices.

Then they found they could store the precious liquid for future use and the numbers that perished dwindled. Each generation from that time forward had their appointed watchers to ensure the storage device was always in good repair and a new one constructed if need be.

Many more started building their own storage devices, thus enabling the community to have that much more of the vital liquid throughout the nau. Now, very few went without and some even had liquid in the devices when the nua returned. But this nau, they would need every bit of precious liquid, and then some, they could collect. They could not afford to waste a single drop.

It had been Grorth who, one sleepless dark time at the beginning of the nau, who heard a loud cracking sound and ventured into the out of doors to investigate. The first thing he saw were the two watchers running past as if their lives depended on getting where they were going; then he saw the crevice in the storage device and as he ran toward it he yelled to anyone he could rouse that there was danger. He knew the crack was not anticipated because he had done the repair check with those entrusted with the duty of watching over the device to learn what they did and how they handled the repairs. The device must have been breaking from the inside from the pressure of the liquid. If they could not contain the spill, many would be without in sixty or seventy rotations. If not sooner. They had to find a way of getting it repaired on both sides, and quickly, with as little lose as possible.

This was the first time anything like this had happened in all of the revolutions Grorth had been on Kladax and he could only think to stop the leak and worry about the rest later. He was met at the storage devise by many members of the community and they all had means with which to collect the escaping liquid. The two watchers arrived breathless and with containers full of what looked like the compound they used to use on Theasos for keeping the sun's heat out of the cooling building for the storage of perishable proteins and the crops. He didn't see why, if it was close to the same thing, it could not also work as a liquid repellent. The two watchers quickly starting putting great amounts into the opening, working quickly but carefully, making sure each amount was smooth and ready for the next amount. Now, they just had to find a way to get to the bottom of the storage device, but from on the inside.

"Grorth?" He turned to see Jloorst rushing toward him. "What if we brought the breathing apparatus that we used when we had to repair the ship? We could bring one of the smaller receptacles of breathing gas and go inside the tank."

"Go!" Now all they had to worry about, after all of this time, was the gas itself. He hoped it was still good. All he could remember his instructor telling him was as long as the receptacles stayed sealed the breathing gas should stay in the tanks. He couldn't remember if they said anything about it staying usable or not. He would soon find out. He would hate to have those standing here get their hopes up, just to dash them with poisonous gas.

Jloorst came lumbering up with a breathing face cover, wet proof light and one of the smaller receptacles dragging behind him. He stopped next to Grorth, took a moment to catch his breath and then quickly put the connectors together and placed the face cover on.

"Oh!" he said as the gas was turned on.

""No good?"

Taking the face cover off, he answered while sputtering and spitting. "Yes, I believe so, but it certainly tastes terrible. I won't be able to stay down long with that taste."

"You stay down?" Grorth couldn't hide his displeasure. As the crew leader, it naturally fell upon his shoulders to undertake the mission. What made Jloorst just assume it would be he that would go? Before Grorth could correct the young officer on his breach of military etiquette, not to mention his plain bad manners, Jloorst spoke.

Looking at his companion, friend and leader, he stated frankly "Grorth, you are newly betrothed and a leader of the community. If we had still been in space, or even at home," and at this point he stopped for a moment and lowered his eyes, the homesickness felt by both, "you would have delegated this work and I most likely would have been the one to do it. I have the training, and let's be honest, who else is crazy enough to do it?"

Grorth looked at him, thought for a moment or two and then said only one word.

"Go."

Hurm, one of the lowest ranking of the crew and without question the shyest, came running up with a suit used with the breathing gas and Jloorst quickly climbed in and Hurm pulled of the closures shut and tight. Grorth thought he had been set up and these two had worked this out before asking his permission, but right now he couldn't worry about that. But, truth be told, he had to laugh at them. He knew they would have found a way to have done it whether he had given permission or not.

Many in the crowd stood in a line and slowly fed the security line and gas hose as Jloorst was lowered into the storage device. Morgos had returned with the medical transporter. Because of the darkness period, someone had put up torches and turned them on full. The area was almost as bright as first sun and it helped settle some of the fears those who watched felt. Someone else had arranged for warmth covers and hot liquids to be ready. There were also nutritional items ready for Jloorst to help revive him. No one there expected him to leave the liquid storage device the same as when he entered, and no one wishes they were in his place.

While everyone waited, the smaller children were returned to their abodes and placed on their sleeping platforms, with the youngest totally unaware they had left the safety of their parents' arms. Each set of parents then agreed to take turns on checking on their smallest family members. No one knew how long Jloorst would be down in the storage device and everyone wanted to be there when he came out. Nothing like this had happened in recent living memory and they all wanted to be part of it, either for the excitement of whether Jloorst would succeed and surface, or not, or for the part all of this would play in the community's history and the bragging ability it provided for many stories in the revolutions to come. Either way, no one was leaving and all had their eyes on the top of the storage device, waiting.

"What if he can't repair it, Umnn?" young Travor asked in his most serious voice. He was asking all of the right questions for his age, but was showing signs of being behind the rest of the children his age group in so many other ways, and Morgos was wondering if Travor was only asking because he had heard other children ask. Morgos remembered how long it took the child to learn his manners and the proper responses that came so naturally to the others. He knew he would have to wait to see, but he was already crushed to think his male child would fall behind the others. Morgos knew all he could do at this stage was encourage the child, and hope the information would take hold.

"If he doesn't," Morgos answered, "we will have to come up with another plan, and quickly." Morgos looked to his beloved. "Is it not time for this young male to be on his sleeping platform and talking with the ghosts of dreams?" He looked down at the child and smiled. He knew his answer wasn't sufficient for the small one, but it would have to do. Morgos just wasn't sure how much he should tell the child, first for his age and second because of the fears the truth would create in such a fertile mind. There would be time to compose a decent answer before morning, when Morgos knew he would be assaulted with questions once again and the child would be more receptive to learning.

"Please, Umnn, may I please stay for only another short while? I, too, am frightened for Jloorst and wish to see him come to the surface safely." What formality the child used when he wanted his way, Anor thought. Why do children learn all of the bad habits first, wondered Morgos. He will, however, make a fine orator in front of the Ruling Council one day with the correct lessons, and that day was not that far in the distance the way Travor was growing and maturing. Morgos hoped for the best and turned his attention back to his male child.

Morgos could not deny his child the request, so he picked Travor up and held him closely. As he suspected, the child was tired and yawned with his head turned from his umnn's gaze, thinking his yawn would not be seen. But the child's body gave him away and he fell asleep on his umnn's shoulder within a very short period of time. Morgos felt a small droplet of moisture leave his eyes and knew he had to put his fears for his male child's future aside for the moment. There were many revolutions to work on the problem and many solutions available. Surely they could find the one that would ensure the small child at least a happy future with his friends.

Jloorst had been down for almost one sixth of a rotation and many were beginning to fear something had gone wrong. Grorth picked up another security line and had it tied around his middle in preparation of going down after his friend. He had decided to give Jloorst just a few more moments and then he was going in when he saw the line coming from the storage device slacken. He dropped his line and picked up the other and started to slowly pull it out of the storage device. Those that had helped to feed it in took hold of their portions of both the security line and gas hose and aided Grorth.

The relief felt by everyone when they saw the gas receptacle come sailing out of the storage device and then a hand reach for the edge was tremendous. The crowd let out such a cheer when Jloorst's head cleared the storage device. He removed the face cover and threw it to the crowd, where Bioux caught it just before it landed on the ground.

"I believe I have it patched tightly."

Cheers, hot liquids, pats on the back and kisses came his way before he had even made it to the ground himself. He was so overwhelmed he did not know what to say and could not have said it if he had the words. Many hands were there to help him out of the suit and Hurm disengaged the gas receptacle and hose. He didn't want to say anything, but the breathing gas was gone. How long it had been like that Hurm did not know, but he hoped not for long, because the face cover would only have enough reserve for a few breaths. Jloorst had cut if far too close for his own safety. Hurm looked up at his friend and the two of them shared a look of common knowledge that they both knew would go no further. Looking back down at the receptacle so he could finish disconnecting them, Hurm had just one thought. Jloorst was crazy. But he loved him as a *vom*, so he would keep their secret.

Many of those there to congratulate Jloorst had not known what else to do, so they had filled many platforms with nutritional items and liquids of all temperatures, so there was enough, in the end, to feed everyone there, and many more, so they turned it into a celebration like no other in recent memory.

The celebration went on long past first sun and on one wanted to leave. When it was time to report to the different workstations and still not that many had left, the Ruling Council's Leader called for quiet.

"As it appears everyone here feels the same, I declare this sun a holiday!" He had to wait even longer for quiet now. When he finally received it, he went on. "Do I hear anyone disagreeing that from this sun forward, we will call this new holiday 'Jloorst Sun'?"

Because he really wasn't all that fond of noise, or celebrations, he headed back to his office. He had so much to catch up on and he felt the festivities were best left to the younger ones. They would not be fit for their workstations until the next sun, and that was fine with him.

The Ruling Council's Leader was at his workstation when the first rays of sun appeared. So much had happened these last few revolutions, he thought - new children, betrothals, emergencies, an invasion, invaders becoming new citizens and new laws, just to name a few. It was the new laws that had him at his workstation and alone in the building.

The people had voted for the very first time and it had been a nice experience but one he didn't plan on repeating. He was old fashioned and didn't hesitate to admit it, but the pressure from those who wanted change was great and he had to be careful how much he did and how fast he did it. He had been elected because he had said the right words at the right time and he had to be careful he did not alienate his supporters. But by his personal time clock, he should have all of this nonsense of voting put behind them by the end of this revolution.

One thing he was happy with, though, was the one very obscure law that allowed him to finish forming Kladax's first ever law enforcement group. He had researched other worlds' law enforcements and they varied so much he felt he could put it together in the manner that suited him the best and no one would complain because they were too *kloomp* to see what was right in front of their faces anyway. Besides, even if they did, he would have the power to stop them. By his reckoning, the law enforcement group would make their first appearance before the citizens were even aware such power was his. He was going to love this career move.

The only problem he could see was Morgos being his next in power. He would try to make him leave first and then if that didn't work he would have to take stronger measures. He knew he could do whatever it took because he was, ultimately, unstoppable.

But there was time. He could afford to take his time and get it right the first time. After all, the public had put him into office for two full revolutions. There was a great deal he could accomplish in that time, especially with the law enforcement group under his total control.

The new law enforcement group made their first appearance with no fan fare and even less publicity, catching the citizens off guard, within the first thirty rotations of the new Ruling Council. They walked down the paths of the community as though no one could stop them, and no one could. The new Ruling Council's Leader had given them total autonomy.

Later that sun, four of them marched into the abode of one of the Ruling Council Leader's biggest opponents and his most vocal critic. The four escorted him to the building and it wasn't until three new suns later that anyone noticed he hadn't been seen since.

Morgos tapped lightly on the entry to the Ruling Council's Leader's office moments after hearing about the disappearance and waited to be invited to enter. He was there to find the answers to two puzzles – since when did Kladax have a law enforcement group and what had happened to his neighbour and friend. He was sure there was some little mix up and the man would make his apologies before the darkness, saying he had been the victim of a joke played on him by his friends in a celebration of one type or another. He was sure it wasn't anything serious, but he had promised to investigate. Then, he saw the members of the law enforcement group for himself coming out of the building as he was entering and realized the disappearance had been real and became determined to get to the bottom of it all.

Morgos did not receive the expected invitation to enter, so he tapped slightly louder the second time and waited once more. It was not until he had tapped the third time that the Ruling Council's Leader asked him to enter. This sort of behaviour, until then, had been unheard of and was considered an affront to the caller. Morgos tried to make the excuse the Ruling Council's Leader had either not heard him, or he had been very busy and could not respond to his first two taps. No matter. He had received the invitation to enter.

Morgos knew next to nothing about the male chosen t lead the people, but he was willing to work with him and Morgos naturally thought some sort of intimacy would come of it. He entered the office with a friendly smile on his face and walked toward the Ruling Council's Leader.

"Quickly, will you?" The Ruling Council's Leader hadn't even bothered to look up. "I have much to accomplish this sun and interruptions like this will just make my rotation that much longer."

Morgos couldn't believe his own ears. Taking a deep breath, biting his tongue and quickly composing his words, he spoke.

"I will make this short, Leader," He hoped the Ruling Council's Leader heard the insult. The Ruling Council's Leader stood no more than twelve teratots high, compared to Morgos' seventeen. "I have heard that one of our citizens has not been seen for some time. People have told me that he was last seen entering your office three rotations ago, and not since."

Angrily, with much hate written on his face, the Ruling Council's Leader interrupted Morgos. Something such as this was unthinkable in the old revolutions.

"And what makes you and your friends think they can spy on me?"

Keeping his voice calm and clear, Morgos answered the Ruling Council's Leader. "We have not been spying, Leader. I am just trying to find a dear friend to many in this community."

Turning his back on Morgos, the biggest insult anyone could inflict on another, the Ruling Council's Leader went back to his work and did not speak again. Morgos didn't waste time to acknowledge his dismissal and turned to leave the office. He also didn't care that he had been equally as rude as the male across the room from him. That guilt would come later, after he had calmed down and rationalized the whole episode from a distance.

"You will not enter this office again unless summoned."

Morgos had stopped in mid step when he heard the Ruling Council's Leader speak but did not turn. Obviously, his insult went over the Ruling Council's Leader's intellectual level. Morgos then continued out of the office and closed the entry softly behind himself. Now was not the time to lose his temper and he would bide his time. He had to find out what was causing this attitude from the Ruling Council's Leader. He had to find out more about the male and quickly. Morgos could smell trouble, big trouble, with this new Ruling Council's Leader, besides his extremely bad manners, and it wasn't going to be easily, or quickly, solved. The new Ruling Council's Leader seemed to think the community was his and his alone to rule and that was what frightened Morgos the most. He headed to the one person he could trust with his feelings, besides his beloved betrothed.

"Grorth", he asked as soon as the entry was closed. He didn't have time to stand on ceremony and he would apologize to his friend later. "What do you know about the Ruling Council's Leader?"

Taking his seat and bidding Morgos to do also, Grorth explained he really didn't know the Ruling Council's Leader that well.

"All I really know is his is new to this part of Kladax. I have been told he came from the other side of the landmass during the last nau. Why do you ask?"

"I just had the most disturbing conversation with him." Morgos took some time to organize his thoughts and then relayed them to Grorth.

"I can't believe someone born of this planet could act in such a manner, no matter what the trouble." Grorth remembered his first rotations on Kladax and the struggle he had learning some of the decorum. He, at least, had an excuse for his behaviour. The Ruling Council's Leader, as far as he could see, did not. And what was with the sudden appearance of the law enforcement group?

"There is a gathering of the Ruling Council during the next dark period." Grorth offered to watch the Ruling Council's Leader during that time and see if he could perceive anything out of the ordinary. It was agreed that the two would then gather at a favourite nutritional centre afterwards and discuss their impressions of the gathering, and of the Ruling Council's Leader.

Morgos took his leave and slowly walked back to his abode, wondering what it all meant and if, maybe, he was seeing too much into a little rudeness. But he did not think so. His family greeted him at the entry and he tried to be cheery and playful as he closed the entry behind him. But Anor could see through the façade. She would speak with him later, after Travor had been put to sleep. Morgos felt like a traitor for agreeing with Grorth's idea but his feelings of guilt and fear were only growing stronger and he had to do something to either put his fears to rest, thus alleviating the guilt or prove his fears right. If he was to prove himself right, he would then have to put things right, and that was what frightened him the most. Morgos had read of past leaders of many worlds who had had power chosen for, or by, them and the evil results. The one that came to his mind quickly was the Emperor of Cenos Five.

He had been elected as Under Statesman and then, within five of their rotations, had murdered his way up the power chain. He found himself at the end of a laser, but not before enslaving his whole peoples and starving more than half of two generations to death in work camps.

Then Morgos' mind went to others who had taken power forcefully and they had all ended with planetary wars. Even the Rnites had the best of intentions when they started out and the whole universe had ended up suffering for their basic needs.

Suddenly, Morgos couldn't stop thinking of several examples of good intentions gone bad or bad intentions causing life to go terribly wrong for the innocent. History had taught him too well and he found he couldn't turn it off. What if the innocent people of Kladax had installed a Sinspinner as their Ruling Council's Leader! Morgos could not sit still to enjoy the nutrition Anor had prepared for him and he found himself pacing the floor of the whole abode, going back and forth and across so many times Anor finally spoke.

"Morgos, please rest. Whatever is bothering you cannot be all that bad." She knew she had spoken far too positively but what else could she do. She still did not know what was bothering her betrothed and she could not come out and ask him. That would have been rudeness not even the most placid of betrothed would abide. She would just have to wait until he was ready to speak with her.

"Oh, Anor, if only you knew what was going through my mind as we speak." He gazed into her eyes and she into his. She saw the tears forming and she felt great sorrow for his unspoken pain. "Even if what I am burdened with turns out to be fact you may never know it all and right now, as much as I wish to, I cannot speak of it."

"Go to your Spiritual Oneness and speak of these things with him, then."

The pain in Morgos' eyes became even greater. "If only I could, Anor. If only I could." He turned away and fell onto the sleeping platform. As much as she didn't want to, Anor had no choice but to leave him there to deal with his pain alone. She settled on the seat in the corner and watched her betrothed. She would be near when he needed her.

They both eventually found solace in sleep, but neither found rest.

The next sun saw both Anor and Morgos long up and little Travor was the last to come to the nutritional platform, where normally he would have been the first and demanding his nutritional items faster than Anor could place them before him. This sun, he found his nutrition already at his place and both of his parents seated. His parents hardly acknowledged his presence and even at his tender age knew there was something serious happening. He also knew he should not bother them and let them address him. As much as he wanted to know, his parents had taught him well to wait until he was informed. He went about enjoying his nutrition, but he kept one eye on his parents the whole while, just in case they wanted to share.

Instead, Travor found his umnn rising from the nutritional platform and putting on his work robes, then leaving the abode. Morgos hardly even gave the customary parting words and he was gone. This frightened little Travor and Anor sat with him, to explain as well as she could. As little as she knew, she imparted this knowledge to the child in a manner in which he would understand to reassure him that all was well in the family unit. This was a most confusing time for not only the child, but also for his parents. Anor just prayed that Morgos would find the peace he needed.

Morgos closed the entry to his abode as softly as he could and started walking slowly toward the building and his employment. He had chosen to retain the career he held before being elected First Assistant to the Ruling Council's Leader, which meant he had to accomplish twice as much in the same work period until he could assign an assistant of his own. He had complained for some time about how boring his work was and how little he actually got to do. Now that he had that, and the work of the First Assistant, he found how much work his profession did entail and he felt guilty about his previous attitude. He made a pact with himself that he would show appreciation to his assistant, when he got one, and would make sure he did not make the poor fellow feel unnecessary, and above all, he would stop complaining about being bored.

He arrived at his office to see his workstation piled high with information discs and requests for immediate action on others. He stood at the entry and stared, then shrugged his shoulders and took his seat. Where to start, he thought. Everyone wanted everything now and almost all of this could wait its turn. He had more important things to do at this time. He reached for the device that allowed him to close and lock his entry from his workstation. This was something he had only done once before in his career and that had been at the bidding of the now retired Streph and it had been for a personal conversation. This time Morgos could not afford to be interrupted while he did what he had to do and as quickly as possible.

When he was sure his entry was secured, he went to work.

Morgos and Grorth entered the gathering room one behind the other and they greeted each other as friends and Ruling Council members do. Had anyone been listening, they would not have thought the two of them had anything on their minds except the forthcoming gathering.

"Morgos, may the darkness period be as good to you as the sun." Grorth held the seat next to him as Morgos put his report discs down.

"I thank you, Grorth. May you have as good a darkness as any sun to date."

They both took their seats after Grorth acknowledge Morgos' greeting just as the Ruling Council's Leader entered. Everyone rose and greeted the Leader.

"Please take your seats. There is much to cover and I do not wish to waste anyone's time."

Formalities over, everyone took their seats and small conversations started throughout the room while notes and reports were readied. Morgos and Grorth spoke of small things and each kept an eye open for any words said that might reflect others felt that danger was close. The gathering was called to order and Grorth motioned to Morgos by prearranged signal that he had heard something. There would be time to talk later.

"The first order of business is the disappearance of some of our citizens," the Ruling Council's Leader began. "I have had reports crossing my workstation," and he looked at Morgos as he spoke, "that one or two of our leading citizens have not been seen for a rotation or two.

"I have had the new law enforcement group look into this matter and they handed me their findings as I was coming to this gathering." The fact that there even was a law enforcement group was news to the majority of the Ruling Council.

"It seems that the citizen called Wahlm was called away to the deathbed of his female sibling. He will be returning after the burial ceremony."

Morgos entered a note into his privacy communication device, turning it slightly so Grorth could read it unobserved.

"As for the citizen known as Flon, he expressed surprise that he was reported as missing. It seems he has spent two or three rotations visiting and has been back at his abode for some time now."

Again, Morgos entered a note and Grorth read it. The two of them had a great deal to discuss later.

The rest of the gathering went without incident and during the break Morgos and Grorth talked with several members of mundane things until they found themselves alone in a corner of the room.

They both knew the gathering room had recording devices everywhere so they were extremely cautious as to what they said.

"Maeho sends her best to Anor and asked that she and Travor spend some time at out abode in the coming days."

"Maeho is very generous of her time and Anor, along with Travor, look forward to the visit. Please extend the same invitation to your beautiful and gracious Maeho."

"Many thank you's. I shall."

They spent the rest of the break along the same lines as did the rest of the Ruling Council. No one who held a seat wished to continue discussing council business during the breaks and it had become a time for honing one's small talk skills. There were always a number of conversations taking place without anything of substance being said.

The gathering was called back to order and the rest of the time was spent on the regulating of the new laws. Morgos and Grorth both listened for subtle references that seemed even a bit out of line and took note of who said what. They both had two or three things to take to their talk later and wished they could end this gathering quickly.

The new law enforcement group needed some guidance with a few rule changes they had brought forth from the old revolutions and there were some on the Ruling Council that thought the group had too much freedom, while others felt they needed more. There was one member who wasn't afraid of the Ruling Council's Leader, and therefore not afraid to press for answers. Had it been anyone else, after what had been happening to the citizens who opposed the Ruling Council's Leader, they never would have gotten away with it. But he pressed on, never backed down, and finally got the answers he was really after.

"Why should they be allowed to enter someone's abode without reason?"

"Do you think they should ask a suspected law breaker if they may enter?" the Ruling Council's Leader rebutted.

"Who should issue their orders?"

"For the time being, I shall."

"I don't like that."

"I do."

"Who should govern the group?"

"Through me, the Ruling Council, of course."

"Through you?"

"Yes. As Ruling Council's Leader, it will fall to me." He knew they didn't like what they were hearing, and at this stage he also knew he couldn't alienate them, so he added "for the time being." He also knew he had one more member of the Ruling Council he would have to take care of, and quickly.

"Why?"

No answer. He felt that question didn't deserve the time it took to even think about, let alone answer.

"When will that change?"

"When the time is right." This *sloo* was getting on his nerves.

"How will we know when the time is right?"

"Because I will tell you when the time is right." He was quickly losing his patience.

"How much freedom do we give them before they become autonomous?"

The Ruling Council's Leader had had enough. It was time to put a stop to it all. He would give them just enough of the truth but not enough that the *kloomps* would have enough strength to remove him from his seat before he had a chance to show them who they were dealing with. He was being forced into showing them more quickly than he thought advisable, but there it was. "They will never be autonomous, but close to it. That way, they can function when the need to, without having to clear their every move with someone."

"Who will they 'clear' things with?"

There was a slight hesitation before the answer. "Me."

"So, no one really runs the group outside of the group?"

"Except me."

The members of the Ruling Council didn't know what to say. They had never been spoken to in such a manner and they needed time to think about what had just happened.

By the time the Ruling Council's Leader adjourned, everyone was tired and just a little overwhelmed with the influx of so much information and confusion, especially the information that they had elected someone who had taken full power over the law enforcement group and this frightened Morgos more than a little bit.

The two friends arrived at the nutritional centre and took a platform where they could keep watch on anyone coming near them from any direction. Grorth felt like a criminal for these actions but soon settled down as they started talking.

"Do you remember learning about people like Stroz, the mad Emperor of Cenos Five, Melnok, the blood thirsty dictator of

Tyrrpanium or Hitler, one of the many who decided they were going to rule Earth?"

"Who could forget?" Grorth shook to remember some of the atrocities these people had done to their own, let alone other planets. "Where are you going with this?"

"First," Morgos answered, "the Ruling Council asked for a means of keeping peace when there wasn't' any real need for it. Next, the new Ruling Council creates a group that has complete control over their own actions and we can't seem to agree on how much freedom they should have. Finally, the Ruling Council's Leader steers the conversation and vote in such a way that a decision is impossible. What was that old earth saying when someone confused the issue with facts?" He hadn't used to for so long, but he knew it would come to him. It was on the tip of his thoughts, and then it did suddenly come to him.

It was a saying he liked to use when speaking of Theasosian politics and one that used to get one member of the Committee in particular very angry. "We were baffled with bullshit, weren't we?"

Trying hard to control his laughter, all Morgos could say was "That we were, my friend. That we were." He took a sip of liquid and then continued. "We were told, without doubt, the Ruling Council's Leader would be the only controlling force with the group until 'the time was right' and that time, my friend, will never come if he gets his way. As far as the Ruling Council controlling the group through the Leader, all he was telling us was is we can say whatever we want but it is only what he tells the group that counts. He could give us any excuse he wants to justify this, too."

The nau had taken hold and many were already feeling the pressure. The heat was the highest it had been in living memory and showed no sign of lessening. Many of the individual storage devices showed themselves to be too small this revolution due higher demand and the second community storage device would not be ready much before the nua. These situations had yet to come up at the Ruling Council gatherings. Nor had the fact that the sanitation system needed replacing before the nua. These were issues that, up until the voting, had been standard items at the Ruling Council gatherings. They would have been dealt with long before the need for them arose. Now, neither Morgos nor any of the carry-overs from the last Ruling Council could get them on the list of items to be discussed. Then there were the issues brought forward by the community on the other side of the landmass. The Ruling Council's Leader had yet to even make a visit to meet these people. They had not even had their representative sworn onto the Ruling Council because he could not travel since the nau. Transport units were not working as they should and the repair crews had not received any orders to correct the problem. It had been sitting on the Ruling Council's Leader's workstation, waiting for a signature, since he himself had been sworn in.

The two friends left the nutritional centre more convinced Kladax was in the hands of a mad adult male than when they had entered. What to do about it was the question because the Ruling Council's Leader had yet to give them a reason to challenge him. He had plausible excuses for each and every failing. That was what made him even more dangerous.

The nau continued and the problems rose. People were starting to scramble for liquid far too early and this left others in a dire situation. They wanted to share, but could not for fear their families would go without later. Meanwhile, many portions of the sewage system had broken down completely. By the middle of the nau, the Liquid Disbursement rule had to be put into use and it had been more that forty revolutions since last being called into service.

Morgos had had about all he could take and he walked into the Ruling Council's Leaders office.

Angrily, he started to shout. "I thought I told you..."

"You did and, until the sun, I have respected your wishes on this matter." Morgos let the Ruling Council's Leader know, by his tone of voice, that he was not one of those who were afraid of him and would confront any challenge the other would throw at him. "But this sun is as far as I can go as far as tolerating you and your inaction when it comes to basic living needs in this community. You and your friends on the Ruling Council have allowed liquid resources to drop to an all-time low and we have had more deaths this nau than ever before due to the lack of proper sanitation."

"I have heard all I wish to hear from you, Morgos." He was trying to call Morgos' bluff. "Please leave this office, and never enter it again."

"Gladly. But first, there is one more thing I will tell you, Leader, and I use that title very briefly. I have talked with the rest of the Ruling Council, who you do not control, and we had decided it is time for you and your friends to go.

"Now, this can be handled in any manner in which you choose, but if you wish to hold your heads up in this community after this sun, I suggest you and your friends step down and move on."

Morgos didn't think the Ruling Council's Leader would ever stop laughing. Morgos stood, respectfully, and waited. When the Ruling Council's Leader did finally manage to stop, Morgos took a step or two back toward the entry and opened it. The rest of the Ruling Council walked in and stood behind him.

"I can show my strength, also, Morgos." He stood and the other entry opened, allowing the law regulation group entry. They entered carrying very old weapons and looking very fierce. "You did not really think I was not going to find out about you and your little group did you? There isn't a thing that goes on in this community that I do not know about ant the sooner you realize that the better for you." The Ruling Council's Leader took a weapon from the closest law enforcement group member and pointed it at Morgos. "You and your little group are more trouble than you are worth, Morgos. I should have all of you 'disappear' like your pitiful friends did."

"I would watch what I said and how loud I said it if I were you, Leader. You never know who might be listening."

Laughing once more, the Ruling Council's Leader took a step closer to Morgos, who stood his ground. "Just who am I supposed to be afraid of, Morgos? You?" He continued laughing, even louder this time. Just as he took another breath to continue his enjoyment, he heard the entry behind him open. He and the law enforcement group members turned as one with surprise written all over their faces.

"Ruling Council's Leader, law enforcement group members, Morgos and friends. How nice to see all of you in one room at the same time." Grorth was standing at the entry, flanked by armed personnel. As they entered the room, several Rnite prisoners followed them.

"Aren't you going to say hello to each other?" Morgos, smiling, asked the Ruling Council's Leader. "After all, you have been keeping each other alive for some time now."

The Ruling Council's Leader was at a loss for words. "How...When...Where....?"

The first Rnite into the room answered the abbreviated questions.

"They found us in the valley where you told us the citizens of Kladax were forbidden to enter. A group of them walked into the valley last sun and right up to our huts as if they knew where to find us. Did you, by any chance, tell anyone we were there, Leader?" He used the title 'Leader' as if it were a dirty word, describing a dirty deed.

"Are you crazy?" shouted the Ruling Council's Leader. "Why would I want to do anything that stupid? You are, or were, the only chance I had of getting rid of those pesky Theasosians and their friends." He started to take a step forward but found a weapon sticking him in his rather ample stomach. He looked down and then took a step backward. He knew those weapons were old, but he also knew they still worked very well.

"Then how did they know we were there, and where to look?"

The Ruling Council's Leader couldn't find an answer quickly enough to that. The first, the very first, thing he had done after swearing his oath of office was to make the valley off-limits to all citizens. He had used the excuse that it was a dangerous place to be and he only had the safety of his people in mind. His supporting evidence for this was the day the boy had fallen down the side of a cliff and had been seriously injured. The Ruling Council's Leader had then moved the Rnites from the caves and into the valley under the cover of the darkness period. There wasn't any way they could have been seen. Who had found them after all of this time, and how?

Turning to the prisoners, Morgos questioned them. "From what ship did you come and when?"

"We will not answer your questions," the same Rnite stated. "We will not answer any questions from any of you."

Looking quite satisfied with that statement, Morgos then said, "Fine. We have someone here that may be able to answer the questions you refuse to answer."

He then motioned to the guards and they surrounded the prisoners and the Ruling Council's Leader. He then stepped into the passageway and disappeared. Everyone kept their places and awaited his return.

Morgos was gone for some time and when he returned he had the three former Rnites with him. He had explained the situation to them and they had gone with Morgos willingly. Curiosity was the main reason, but to maybe meet a family member or friend was the strong drawing card. They followed Morgos into the room and as they pushed past everyone they found the other Rnites sitting at the platform with their hands tied behind them and a cord around their waists, as called for by the ancient customs.

"Cau?" Codid asked, with complete bewilderment. "Is that you, my long lost brother of choice?" He walked up to the smallest of the captured Rnites and leaning over, he stared into the other's face. "It is you, is it not?"

The Rnite hung his head. Everyone took that as a sign of identification.

Standing, Codid explained. "This is Cau, my brother by choice. He was in need of a family unit as a small child and we provided such for him. As the years passed, we became as true brothers, as well as good friends.

"When the situation on our home world became common knowledge, Cau and I, along with many of our friends, signed up to go on the search for cerium. We had been told we could mine it, with the permission of the different planets peoples, and no one would suffer for it. Renos was to send as many as thirty ships to each known quadrant and begin collecting immediately so we would all be back before the change of seasons. We believed what we had been told. Why would we not? Thus, Cau and I were assigned to different ships and different quadrants so we have not seen or heard of each other since leaving Rnos.

"We were allowed to voice each other but once and that was at the beginning of our journeys." Looking at his chosen brother Codid put his hand on the other's shoulder. "Why are you here and hiding like wanted animals, Cau?"

Before Cau could provide an answer, the Ruling Council's Leader rushed ahead and screamed at Cau. "Don't say a word! They can't prove a thing!"

Morgos looked at several watchers to the scene playing out before him and decided to clear the room. He was thinking that if the two brothers by choice could speak along for a while they might learn more than treating Cau as the prisoner he presently was. Morgos had no idea if it would work in real life, but it certainly did in all of the ancient texts he had been studying since joining the Ruling Council.

"I want this room cleared, please." Before he could explain why, the Ruling Council's Leader shouted at him.

"Who put you in charge? Have you forgotten who I am?"

"No one put me in charge," Morgos said quietly. "It is just a fact that someone had to take charge and since no one else seemed interested in doing so, I took it upon myself to act as leader at this time." The Ruling Council's Leader didn't need it spelled out for him. He was done. Morgos then turned and showed a group toward the main entry while the guards took the prisoners through the other. Morgos asked them to leave Cau where he was. Codid realized immediately what Morgos was thinking and he walked up to Morgos, head hung slightly down.

"I thank you, Morgos. You are a good friend and a good leader."

Patting Codid on the shoulder, Morgos walked over to Cau and undid the bindings that held him to his seat. He then held his hand out to Cau. Cau looked suspiciously at Morgos and then glanced at Codid. Codid smiled at his brother by choice and then, rising to his feet, Cau took the hand that was still held out to him. Morgos then smiled at the two and quietly left the room, closing the entry behind him. He motioned two guards to stand at each side of both entries and instructed them to allow no ne entry into the room.

"If either wishes to leave, that is their prerogative. But no one is to interrupt them for as long as they need." Morgos then went over to Datron and Znow to ensure them they could wait in the passageway for their friend. He made sure they had everything they might need and some things they would have no need for even in their own abodes.

Morgos then went to find Grorth and the other former Theasosians. There was much to discuss with the Ruling Council, but it could all wait. Morgos just wanted to be with friends for a short while and put what had transpired to the back of his mind. There would be plenty of time to deal with all of it later. He knew the one thing he was procrastinating on and that was the one thing that hurt him the most. As First Assistant to the Ruling Council's Leader, it was for him to formally take the Leader into custody and try him for treason, among many other charges. Morgos had never like the Leader, but this was far more serious than personality differences. He may have to put the current Ruling Council's Leader to death. If that was the wish of the court. Just the thought of it made Morgos shudder and left him with a bad taste in his mouth. He was not prepared for any of this. He wasn't even sure he had the heart for it. Maybe they would just put the Leader away for the rest of his life. Morgos could only hope.

Morgos found the remaining members of the Ruling Council waiting for him at the main entry to the building. They all started asking him questions as soon as they saw him approaching and he called for quiet.

"We won't know anything until the conversation is over. I have asked the guards to voice me when it is and then we will hear the report together."

"Morgos?" The voice was so quiet Morgos knew it could only be Smun.

"Smun?"

The quiet little Smun knew everyone was watching him and waiting to hear what he had to ask and it embarrassed him. He did not like everyone looking at him, making him the centre of attention. But what he had to say was so very important.

"The Rnite who says the least is the one to watch most carefully and closely."

There. He had said it.

"Why is this, Smun?" Morgos was most gentle with Smun and made sure they made eye contact only with each other. Morgos hoped this would relax the timid Smun and help him speak his news with as little fear as possible.

"When we were standing in the room, waiting for you to return, Morgos, I heard the Rnites speaking about protecting this other one at all costs." Coaxing him gently, Morgos heard about Cau's importance and whatever was in the valley either had great value or, as Morgos suspected, could do greater damage to Kladax itself. Smun believed whatever it was Cau knew how to use it. Morgos thanked the little Smun and put his hands on both of Smun's shoulders. His thoughts went to Codid at that moment. He must be in an awful place at this moment. He has adopted Kladax as his home, but he is still, and always will be, a Rnite. What must he be thinking and how must he be feeling was of great concern to Morgos and he made a mental note to speak with Codid as soon as possible.

"I will send an emissary to the valley immediately to locate and investigate this secret hiding place. Whatever it holds, we have you to thank for imparting your news to us."

Smun was just grateful the attention would finally be on someone else and he could go back to be as near to invisible as any living being could get.

The private conversation between Codid and Cau was an emotional one and they both felt more than a little disjointed with each other. Much had changed in their lives and the found they now no longer truly knew each other. They may both still be Rnites by birth, but life had changed the reality of that, at least for Codid. He took a seat next to his brother by choice and good friend.

"What happened, brother? Tell me what has happened to you these long revolutions since I last heard from you."

Cau sat with his head down and Codid saw the first of what were to become many drops fall from Cau's eyes. Never had Codid seen him so miserable, not even when they had first found him alone, cold and half starved in the middle of the darkness period. Codid remembered it as if it were the last rotation, instead of almost thirty revolutions. After they had given him some nutrition and a hot liquid, followed by restful sleep, they asked him what had put him out of his family abode and love circle.

"I was not wanted and my family had always made me understand and accept that." He was showing the resignation of his situation on the maturity level of one much older than he. To hear him speak of these things was like listening to him recite a list of needs from a product dispenser. "My female parent did not have a mate and she had told me that I would have to find my own way when I had reached ten revolutions of age. I did not wait that long. She would leave me alone for many rotations without nutritional items or drinkable liquid and then become angry upon her return when I told her how hungry I was.

"So, not long after I had reached five revolutions, I started teaching myself how to steal nutritional items and I became quite good at it. At least I thought I was. One nutritional supplier would be kind to me and just hand me things, but I don't know if he knew I was stealing from him, also, or not, or if he just took pity on me.

"Anyway, I was stealing a warmer clothing item when the man who owned the clothing centre caught me and started chasing me. I was trying to hide from him when you," and he pointed to Codid's male sibling, "found me. I thought you were going to turn me in, but you were kind to me and now here I have become a burden to others outside of my family circle." He started to rise to leave and the female parent of the abode placed her hand on his shoulder and gently pushed him back into his seat.

"You are here to stay and you are not a burden until we say you are." Looking into the young child's eyes, she asked "Where did someone of your tender revolutions learn such a big word, anyway?"

Cau's eyes were still moist and the moisture was finding its way down his cheeks even faster. "My female parent said 'Burden' should have been my other name. I have been called other names by her but Burden is the nicest one."

Codid's male parent asked if there were other children at his old abode.

"I am number three of five. She wanted all of them except me, I guess."

"Why you? What was so different between you and the rest that she would only not want you?" Codid's male parent was on the verge of a terrible rage and all could feel it. If there was one thing he hated the most, it would be someone not treating their child like the gift he or she was. Even if the expected child had not been planned or even wanted, once they were there they became the responsibility of the parents, no questions asked. There wasn't any room in society for expendable offspring. He knew of many who wanted, but would never have, children of their own and that was the way it was. You just did not take another's and raise them. But when they showed up on your abode's front entry that was different.

Cau hung his head once more and moisture fell into his lap. "I am the only one to be born to her that would not reap her much money from the male parent. She had made the mistake of becoming with child by a male without money or social standing. She saw me not as a child but as one who could not put fancy things on her back and money in the depository. I was a drain on her finances and the money the others brought to her. Since he could not give her money, he could not provide for me, so I was cast aside. So, I left on my desires, not hers."

No one in the room had a dry eye, but there was much they still needed to know. "How long have you been out there on your own?" Codid's male parent was afraid of the answer, but he knew he had to hear it.

"I left my female parent's abode not long after my sixth summer and I have been gone for almost a full revolution now."

He was seven summers and looked as if he could not be more than four. It would take a great deal of love and good nutrition to help him thrive. It was something the whole family wanted to do, so they put his name above the entry with the others. He was officially a member of this abode and nothing was ever going to change that.

Now here he was, many revolutions later, once again lost and confused. He was grateful Codid was not angry with him.

"I found out soon after we left Rnos that we had been lied to. It did not matter how much cerium we took from a planet it would leave it destroyed and in some cases non-existent. I felt that to be so wrong and made the mistake of speaking out to others about how I felt. My leader found out and put me in locked seclusion for the rest of our mission. We had followed the trail from the Theasosian ship and it led us here. We were staging a raid to capture the Theasosians when we lost altitude and crashed in the valley where we were found.

"When we took count of who had survived, there were so few of us and I was the only one who knew how to use the weapons we had built from the damaged ones for the raid. Only a handful of us knew there wouldn't be much of a planet left when we were finished, but we had convinced ourselves that the Theasosians had done us a grievous wrong and we were correcting it. Even I bought into it, thinking it was war and we never lost. When I had discovered what the weapon would do to Kladax, I had reached the point where I was no longer convinced it was war but just brutality and I wanted nothing to do with it. But my leader was one of those who survived the crash and he had threatened me that if I did not get the weapon working he would stand over me with a disruptor and make sure I did and then he would make sure I was strapped to the weapon when it went off.

"Either way, no matter what I did, I was dead.

"Now, I will stand trial and face whatever punishment the Kladaxions hand me. It will be rightly deserved. Then, if I should be so fortunate as to be sentenced to punishment instead of eternal rest, I will do my time with honour and try to be a good citizen of wherever I should be upon my release. I am tired of war, fighting and killing. I just want to be at peace and live until Olag finds it time to call me." He looked at Codid with questions written in his eyes.

"I don't think that will be much of a problem, brother. But let's get the trial over with first, and then we will make definite plans for your future." He clasped his brother's hand and they both rose to their feet, hugging each other for the first time since that darkness period when Cau had joined his new family unit.

They then turned and walked to the entry, ready to face what awaited them on the other side.

The entry to the gathering room opened and the waiting crowd slowly crept forward. They looked at the two brothers, sitting side by side, but could not tell how they were feeling. Those that could find seats did so and the rest lined the room three and four deep. No one wanted to miss a thing, especially if it meant the fall of their government. That had not happened in over a thousand revolutions, and even that one had not been necessary, as history taught.

Morgos entered with the guards and prisoners close behind him. There was an audible intake of breath from the crowd when they saw that the Ruling Council's Leader was also bound.

Morgos did not look al the crowd as he climbed the raised platform's steps. In all of the revolutions this room had replaced the old, no one had had reason to climb those three steps except to clean the platform. This would be the first official duty on this level for Morgos and for the Punishment Platform. Morgos hoped no one could see, or hear, his shaking and knocking knees. He wished he knew someone with the illegal intoxicant liquids. He could use some right about now.

He turned and faced the assembled friends, neighbours and loved ones he had known all of his life. The room was packed and once again the peopled flowed out into the passageways and into the streets. Word of what had happened, and what may yet come to be, had not taken long to spread throughout the community. The very nervous, and truly upset, Morgos waited until everyone had seen him and total quiet was achieved. I would love to be anywhere but here, he thought as he stood as tall as he could and prepared to speak.

"The remaining members of the Ruling Council sent a representative to the valley and this agent found the secret hiding place. I will now ask the emissary to come forward and inform all gathered this sun to report what was found."

The back entry opened and all waited to see whom this emissary was. Then, as he entered, there was total silence for a short period and then gasps, ooh's and shocked intakes of breath.

Entering the room was Grorth's personal robot from off his ship and two more just like it.

The robots joined Grorth and turned toward the crowd. All was still silent. No one had seen any of the service robots since the ship had landed and they were put into silence mode. For many, this was their first exposure to the robots in active mode and to others their first sight of them at all.

They didn't really look like much, many thought. They weren't much beyond a long, narrow circular thing with an almost insect-like head. Their arms and legs were very narrow and made of a strong metal with two claw-like appendages used for grasping at the end of what would be its arms. They stood on two almost square and thick blocks that would have been feet, and they had independent movement just like feet. One girl child whispered to her female parent they looked almost like the insect she had studied in educational groups the Earthlings had called a mantis. Her female parent quickly hushed her and turned her attention back to the platform, but she silently agreed with the child. Large, but a mantis just the same. Instead of wings, the robots had huge power packs and voice emitters on their backs and they looked quite tame, really, and moved with surprising smoothness. They were, in many ways, ugly but no one could take their eyes off them. For some unknown reason, they captured ones attention, and held on to it. It was almost scary. Grorth motioned to one of the robots to begin.

"We were sent into the valley because what awaited anyone who entered was unknown." The robot's voice was very mechanical, yet somewhat very familiar to all. It sounded almost as any of them did. "I am equipped with bomb sensing devices and full self-protection capabilities. Therefore, it was logical to send me instead of a living being with the other two to assist me. I have had these protective measure removed prior to entry to this room.

"I scanned the valley for any incendiary devices and honed in on just one. My sensors informed me this to be a class ten photon device, capable of destroying this complete planet if activated.

"I then disarmed this device and returned to base.

"End of report."

The robot then moved to the back of the platform and went into wait mode with the others.

The silence that followed was profound and everyone in the room could feel the ill will against not only the Rnites who had been captured but also their own Ruling Council's Leader.

According to the ancient texts Morgos and read, the Leader was now entitled to verbally defend himself. Morgos asked the guards to bring the Leader forward to the platform.

The Ruling Council's Leader fought the arms of the guards but was overpowered and made to climb the steps. He then was turned to face his people He stood there, head bowed, for some time and then with a defiant look upon his face, he looked out at the crowd and spoke.

"It was a matter of survival. It turned into war and I chose my side." He looked out at his fellow Kladaxians and shouted "You would have done the same thing if you had been me!" He started to weep. "All the Rnites wanted to do was live! These Theasosians and the traitor Rnites had to die. Don't you see? If they lived, they would forever be a reminder of the failure of a complete race! By their deaths, and the deaths of the victorious Rnites, the race would go down as winners! As the powerful people they are! Can't you see what my helping them would do for this planet? We would be remembered as a people who cared enough to help! Can't you see that?" The Ruling Council's Leader was sobbing uncontrollably.

A lone voice, that of a young male adult, came from out of the crowd.

"By whom would we be remembered, Leader? By whom?"

The Nua

The nua came and with them the public guilt assessment of the former Ruling Council's Leader. The newly formed Ruling Council and its new Leader had had to work overtime to ensure everything was in readiness for the nua and the new sanitation system was completed. Morgos, Grorth and the rest of the members of the Ruling Council learned what hard work really was during this time and they loved it. They had come to realize what a soft life they had been living and decided to change their ways. It was decided that each member of the Ruling Council would go out into the field and spend some time with the workers, hands on, to get a better appreciation and understanding of what it took tom make the community function.

Then, they turned their attentions to the guilt assessment.

Morgos had spoken with Codid about his feelings of what had happened to Cau and what could happen soon. Codid was torn between being a Rnite and also a Kladaxian. He was a Kladaxian by choice but his Rnite roots were still deep. He hated to see Cau in trouble but he also knew his brother by choice would face it like a man. He had no animosity toward the Kladaxions but the Rnites were another matter. No matter what the circumstances, no Rnite treated another the way Cau's leader had done. Codid would have to learn to live with that, but he found it extremely difficult at this stage.

It had been so many centuries since a guilt assessment had been heard on Kladax that the Ruling Council had to study and learn the ancient texts and form the appropriate branches of government and train them in their new employment and responsibilities. They then had to educate the public on the functioning's of all these so they could follow the proceedings with comfort and knowledge.

By the time all of this had been accomplished, along with the preparations for the nua, the first moisture was felt. Excitement went through the community and the celebrations of the end of the nau went on all darkness and into the new sun. There seemed to be a new feeling of security to the community and a feeling of oneness.

Several people mentioned to Morgos it was almost like having Streph back as Ruling Council's Leader, but somehow different.

Morgos was honoured and promised each and every citizen the freedom to speak with him at any time. There were going to be some changes on the Ruling Council and how it functioned and the first changes would come from the top.

When the people had first approached Morgos about letting his name stand for Ruling Council's Leader he had felt it was only because of the leadership role he had taken in the arrest of the old Ruling Council's Leader and the outlaw Rnites. Then Maeho sat him down and told him a few plain facts of life.

"These people have know you all of your life, Morgos. Do you really think they would base their opinion of you on one act? They put their trust in you, and not for the first time, when they asked you to sit on the Ruling Council and that was because they knew the kind of being you are.

"They put their trust in you, without question, when you told them what was needed to get us through the nau. They never even questioned that you may or may not have known what you were doing. They just did as you asked of them and your actions got us through that hard time.

"Now you act surprised they want you as their leader."

Morgos did not know what to say, except his betrothed was correct. It was still hard for him to accept but he must find a way. He must find a way of accepting these accolades without embarrassment. It was not the way in which he had been raised and therefore they did not settle well with his personal code of conduct. He had had leadership skills all of his life and they had meant very little. Now he would be using all he had, and more, for some time to come. He just hoped he could measure up to the expectations of his fellow citizens.

The sun that those who would serve as adjudicators were assembled came at a time when there were so many other things to do, but those who had been called went with a sense of pride. There would be nineteen all told to hear the words of all sides and make a decision as to what would happen to those that faced guilt assessment. There wasn't any recourse for those who were obviously guilty or who pled guilty after their arrest and before their assessments. They would all have to stand up for guilt assessment and because their crimes were all the same, they would stand together and hear their rulings together.

The one who would indicate the guild assessment findings was a difficult position to fill. No one wanted to tell the community if things went in favour of those who stood for assessment. This position became the responsibility of a senior member of the community called Bandl. He had been a student of Kladax history his whole life and there wasn't anyone who thought they could do a better job of being fair.

The hardest portion of the process was finding someone to stand up for the accused during the proceedings. There wasn't a person in the community that wanted the post and no one could blame them. So it fell to Jloorst, the only person nominated, to serve as volunteer champion.

The next hardest was the accuser. This person would represent the community and would present the charges against the accused and the case that supported those charges. This fell to another community leader with a solid reputation and standing named Thern.

But when it came to finding someone to serve as overseer, the people of Kladax lined up. Morgos was pleased at this point that everyone involved with the process had to have special training in the laws and procedures because once this was common knowledge, the waiting list to serve shortened to within easily handled numbers.

The sun the guilt assessment started found the special room full to capacity and once again people lined the passageways of the building and others were standing outside, listening and watching the monitors. The one they had all come to hear speak was the last to enter the room, the former Ruling Council's Leader known once again as Tae. He entered with his head held high and a look of confidence on his face. He followed the rest of the accused to the enclosure and sat down with a rod straight back. He even looked the slightest bit bored with it all. It has to be his arrogance, many thought. He can't really be thinking this is just a frivolous action that is wasting his time and he is going to be supported in his actions. Olag forbid.

"This guilt assessment will begin," shouted a guard and Bandl entered the room with the overseer behind him. Many strained their necks to see who had taken such a difficult post but no one was really all that surprised. The position had gone to Streph.

The guard settled the crowd down quickly and the guild assessment started. The champion was allowed to speak first on behalf of his clients and everyone who knew him knew how hard that was for him, but he never let any of his feelings or emotions show themselves. He knew he had to appear to everyone there to be on the side of the accused in order to do his job properly.

"The champion will now speak."

Jloorst rose to his feet and slowly turned to face the adjudicators, then the overseer and finally the observers. He may have been able to hide his emotions, but he couldn't hide the fact that he was nervous, extremely nervous. He may be accustomed to power and giving others orders but this was totally new to him and out of his realm of expertise.

"Overseer, Accuser, Indicator, observers. These men before you are being accused of crimes against not only the people of Kladax but also the whole universe as we once knew it." There were several intakes of breath and a few ooh's and ah's heard from around the room. Where was Jloorst going with this?

"The Rnites only did what they must in order to survive. At what juncture would you stop trying to save your own lives, and your world? Tae, out of his own sense of decency, did what he felt what was right." He paused for a moment, waiting for the room to cease before continuing, and looked at his clients. "As did the former Ruling Council's Leader. After hearing Cau's story, I would like you to put yourselves into his soul place and ask if you would do anything different. Then ask yourself if you would not do as the former Ruling Council's Leader had, for he, also, felt he was doing what he had to in order to protect his life and those of his world."

He paused once again and looked at each and every person in the room and then into every screen before continuing.

"I somehow don't think so." He walked over to the judicators and looked at each one, one at a time, and then went to his seat. Before sitting, he said one more thing.

"If it is evidence you seek, then search your own souls and hearts."

Thern then rose to speak.

"Overseer Streph, Champion Jloorst, judicators, observers. This is a straightforward case. These criminals," and he pointed to the cage, sweeping his hand across to encompass them all, "are guilty of the crimes for which they are being assessed here this sun. There is no question about that and therefore they must be found guilty and dealt with according to law." He had no finesse and no concern about following the rules of the assessment. He was going to do the job his way. He felt by his age alone he had earned that right. "The law states that I must present evidence to you. So I shall give you evidence. After seeing what I have as evidence, there will be no doubt." His opening was more of a summing up, but he didn't care. This was his moment, and he would use it to show everyone how intelligent, and great, he really was and how by having him as accuser they couldn't have chosen any better than him. He was going to set a precedent for the job that wouldn't be matched for generations to come and he could do it because he was unequalled in any phase of life.

He took his seat, smirked and adjusted his robes confident he had just won his case.

Overseer Streph called a short break so the parties involved could prepare for the next phase of the guilt assessment – that of asking questions of seers and the presentations of any and all evidence pointing toward guilt by Thern and innocence by Jloorst. Those who usually would have placed a wager on the outcome of the guilt assessment were silent this sun. They knew in their hearts it would have been a waste of time and money. Besides, who would take their bids? The outcome was a guarantee. They would have bet on it.

After the break, Thern rose and presented his case against the accused. He called as his first seer the male parent of the boy child who discovered the Rnites hiding in the valley. Because of the child's age, he was forbidden to appear and his male parent was to speak for him.

"Zlorn, tell us what your child related to you."

The male parent was upset and he knew by relating the story to those assembled he would be putting his disgrace on the open platform for all to see. But he also had to tell his male child's story for justice to be done. He knew he was among friends but to have one's disgrace aired in public was a humiliation that would burn in him forever.

"My child, like every other child in the community, knows to stay out of the forbidden valley. But, also as other children, does not understand why the valley is forbidden and his curiosity took over his sense of good behaviour and he went to see what the secret was." The male parent took a deep breath and continued before he lost his nerve. This was so hard. Maybe the hardest thing he had ever done in his life. He was just grateful the law didn't allow the child to do this. Even in his innocence, he would have broken down under the strain of admitting his committing such a breach of etiquette.

"He found abodes where no abodes should be and as he walked closer he saw who he thought was a friend. He had not seen a friend. He had found not his friend Datron but another Rnite. A stranger.

"The child then came to me and confessed his bad behaviour and accepted his punishment. My family unit is now disgraced by his actions and we will bear our disgrace as well as we can. We are grateful the community has not, as in the long ago past, banished us for the actions of a curious child."

Overseer Streph then said the words only he, as final overseer in all things connected to the case, could. They room was silent in support of those long awaited words.

"Zlorn, it pleases me to inform you, in the presence of the community, that your shame has been lifted and you and your family unit are once again full members of a loving, caring society. Granted, what your male child did was wrong but it was the end results of what he did that count this sun. Because of the bravery of the child to tell you, instead of hiding the truth, for which you and your betrothed must be commended for teaching the child, we are here this sun to bring these accused criminals to their guilt assessment before any harm could come to this community. For that, we owe your male child our gratitude, not our condemnation."

Zlorn rose, bowed to Streph, the accuser, the adjudicators and the observers. He then left the room with moisture falling from his eyes. The silence in the room stood until long after the entry had closed behind the grateful male parent. It took all present a moment to clear their own eyes of the accumulated moisture that some had not been able to prevent from falling. Streph then called for Thern to call his next seer.

"I wish to have Morgos come forward and tell his story."

Morgos rose and adjusted his robes. He had prepared for this sun and wanted to be at his best. This was his chance to find some of the long awaited relief over this whole episode he had been seeking. He stepped forward and presented his story.

"If the valley," he concluded, "had not been forbidden, the crews working on the sanitation system could have completed their work in half the time and then gone on to other pressing things. But because no one was allowed into the valley, they had to prepare a new receiving station and processing system, which meant the sanitation system was not ready for the nua and we experienced flooding for the first time in many generations.

"When I approached the then Ruling Council's Leader to seek permission for the crews, I was told not to ask again. I had already been banished from the Leader's office and only allowed in when asked. So when I entered without invitation all I ended up doing was enraging him even more. Now, to this day, we do not speak and the feelings we have for each other border on intense dislike, which goes against all that I was raised to believe in. For this, I have deep sorrow."

The indicator used the better part of three rotations presenting his case and then it was the turn of the champion. Jloorst called his first seer. Tae.

"I had heard the stories," Tae said, "of how the leaders of Rnite had lied to those who served aboard their ships. I had heard why they ventured out into space and the need that drove them there. I had also heard how many societies perished because of the Rnite's search for cerium.

"But I also put myself in their place and asked what I would have done if the people of Kladax had such a need. What would I have done to ensure their survival and continued good health? I had only one answer. I would have done the very same thing.

"Granted, lying as to how much damage would have been done and the number of lost souls was not such a good thing, but the Rnites needed cerium and they were going to acquire it, no matter what. Just because you don't believe in killing anyone does not mean you yourself must die of starvation, does it? I think not.

"So, when I received that faint transmission several revolutions after the end of the conflict, I had not choice but to help. I knew they would not be welcome in the community so I arranged for them to settle in the valley and so they would not be disturbed until they were ready to be presented to the community, I had the valley ruled forbidden.

"Yes, I knew the Rnites would seek out their own who had turned their backs on them and those they had fought against and had escaped. I knew those the Rnites sought would loose their lives. But please believe me when I state that I had no idea they had planned on killing us all. I truly did not know this for if I did I would not have aided them at all. I had been told they would take just what they needed to regain good health and a little for their journeys and then they would leave." He paused for a moment, regaining his emotions that had threatened to break loose. "I can't believe I fell for their lies, also. What a fool I have been."

All of the Rnites in the enclosure, except one, had nasty smirks on their faces and did nothing to try to disguise them.

Jloorst called his second, and final, seer, Cau. He related what had happened since crash landing on Kladax and the threats he had received from his own leader.

"Once I discovered we had been lied to," he said, "I only wanted to find my way off the ship and return home. I knew what I wished to do was treason and desertion, but I ceased to care. We had been sent out to destroy other worlds, without any feeling or caring about the habitants of those worlds, in order for the ruling class to live. We, of the working class, may or may not even have benefitted from these actions, and I wanted nothing to do with it. But I was trapped. I had to follow orders and when we landed here, I knew escape to be impossible for there was no where for me to go. I must admit my sense of relief when we were finally discovered and brought here to the community. At least the inhabitants of this planet, and the planet itself, would survive." The rest of his testimony was equally emotional and many observers felt he should not be found guilty as the others. They hoped Streph would give the judicators this as a choice. Many doubted he would as it was not called for under the law, but they still hoped for it.

The rest of the guilt assessment was short and the proceedings finished within two rotations of Tae's statement. The adjudicators sat for only one portion of a rotation and then presented their findings and decisions to the overseer.

The number one adjudicator rose and handed the decision to Bandl.

"Overseer, the adjudicators have found all of the accused guilty of the charges against them." The assembled crowd started to complain loudly and the Overseer had to bring them back to order, which was not an easy feat. When it was finally accomplished, Bandl continued. "However, they also find special influences on the part of Tae led him to the actions he undertook.

"Therefore, even though guilty of the charges, they find him not responsible." The cheering was so loud, the Overseer chose to wait until the crowd had it out of their systems, and then Bandl finished reading the statement before him. "They believe he was also a victim of the Rnites and their lies. They believe had he seen through those lies sooner, he would not have done what he did.

"They also find special influences on the part of Cau. Had he felt like a free person to make choices, they would have found him guilty along with the others of Rnos. But since he himself was a prisoner, of sorts, he did not. They find a prisoner of choice to still be a prisoner. Therefore, they find him only partially responsible. They thank the Overseer for this time."

The room erupted into shouts and many were brought, by their anger, to using language unfit for ears anywhere. The crowd had wanted, Tae found responsible and felt cheated. Streph brought them back under control and then delivered his judgement.

"Defendants. Please rise." They each rose to their feet and some knees were not up to supporting the weight placed upon them and help was required to keep these few on their feet.

"You have been found guilty of the crimes charged against you. Therefore, according to law, I impose your sentences.

"Rnites, you are outworlders and therefore our laws do not speak to your circumstances. Therefore, I must consider whether to treat you as Kladaxians or wait until new law is written.

"Since I was not empowered to make new law this sun and the wait would be unreasonable for all concerned, I will sentence you as Kladaxians. Such is the way of Kladax.

"All of you will be sentenced to life servitude in the valley. You will live, work and survive there, alone. You will not enter the community you set about to destroy and no one from the community will go into the valley unless specifically requested by the law enforcement group." There had been no concessions made for Cao. Codid felt bad for him, but knew he would face his punishment as he said he would. There just would be no future life for him in the community.

The Overseer then addressed Tae.

"Had it not been for your greed and misguided sense of right and wrong you would most likely have seen through the Rnites lies and what they had planned for Kladax. You would not have been in such a hurry to believe we would have survived and gone on our way. You most of all, through your haste and inability to reason the situation, will receive the harshest of sentences.

"Tae, you will live at the other end of the valley and only communicate with others in emergency. Your time will be spent alone, without the comfort of friends and family. When you time comes, you will be laid to rest where you fall."

Such was the sentence that the overseer had imposed and Tae got his wish in the end. The valley truly was forbidden. It was also the one and only prison on Kladax. Those sentenced to live there would work as sanitation workers and learn to grow their own crops and make their own abodes liveable. The law enforcement group would rotate shifts and ensure the sentences were carried out and certain living standards were met. If the Rnites had difficulty with basic needs, they were to be met until a way was found for the Rnites to provide for themselves. No one in the valley would, as in days past, be allowed provisions from the community to see them through the nua. Tao would not be allowed such simple pleasures as working with others again. His life would be a solitary one.

The room soon empted of observers, officials and guards. Each returned to their lives, except the Rnites and Tae of course. They were transported immediately to the forbidden valley to begin their sentences. Fortunately for the Rnites, their abodes still stood. Tao had to start from the beginning and to do so in the middle of the nua was not easy feat. His clothing and personal items were transported to him, as were the nutritional items he had in his old abode. A small liquid storage device was also supplied while he built a larger, more permanent one. He would also have to figure out how to build a sanitation system before too much longer as he wasn't connected to the community's services. The community also provided a temporary shelter to shield him from the nua and the blazing sun that would follow. This protection would be taken away within a few very short rotations and unlike his fellow prisoners he had never build even a rudimentary cover. His abode had been prepared for him and he didn't have a clue how to go about even starting one. It was going to be a difficult time for him, but he couldn't waste any worrying about it.

Life returned to normal in the community for the rest of the citizens. Little ones grew and older ones died. Middle ones became betrothed and had more little ones. Grorth and Naeho started their family. For someone who, at one point in his, thought he would never find happiness let alone bonding, the fact that he was about to become a parent was more contentment than he could contain within himself. The naming ceremony was attended by all, including two of Naeho's former suitors who thought, or maybe hoped, her bonding would never last. They were the first to present the child with gifts of love.

It came as not surprise to the celebrants when the parents presented the child and vocalized the chosen name.

"From this day forward," Grorth proudly stated, "our girl child shall be known as Wahon, in memory of those so recently lost to us." The cheers showing the approval of the crowd were as loud and as long as they could be. Their friends would not be forgotten and their memory would live through this small child. Everyone was in agreement that Wahlm and Flon would have been proud, also and Naeho and Grorth couldn't have done a better thing.

The new Ruling Council made sure everything was in readiness when the nua came to a close for the beginning of the nau. The liquid storage devices were full and well maintained. The proper amount of nutritional pellets were dispersed to each abode for emergencies and all abodes had the necessary coolant available for the middle of the nau.

Morgos and his Ruling Council then called a community gathering. There were one or two new changes yet to be made public and they felt the community would be pleased to hear them.

"We, the Ruling Council of Kladax," Morgos announced, "will be known simply as the Council. We felt that to have the title of Ruling Council was too dictatorial and all-encompassing.

"Secondly, the place of birth will no longer be a consideration when applying for eligibility for Council. Everyone now living in freedom on Kladax and of proper age is eligible.

"Third, Grorth has an announcement."

"As of the next sun," Grorth said, "the ship upon which we arrived will be destroyed." Several in the crowd showed signs of surprise and some even of shock. Many of the younger ones had grown up never knowing a ship not to be in orbit.

"We have taken all we can from the ship and now there is no reason to keep it. We are home and home to stay." He caught his voice as it started to crack and then continued. "If, in some distant future, there is a reason to venture out into space once again, we will start fresh.

"There are good, and bad, memories aboard that ship for those of us who served on her, but now it is the time to say good-bye. But there are one or two robots we have chosen to keep active and you have met them. They are the ones who served as emissaries to us in the forbidden valley. The rest of them will be returned to storage and maybe find a place amongst us one day.

"Finally, and most important, I have been researching other worlds and their ways of containing liquids during their nau. I understand from our engineers that cutting into the surface of the planet is most difficult due to its hardness of top and brittleness of its interior. However, I believe we may have a way of doing it.

"We on Theasos, among many, developed a compound that hardened when dry and they would line holes of various descriptions and uses, thus trapping liquids inside. Now, I know this is nothing new here on Kladax and such things have been used for millennia. But what if we were to dig down below the brittle layer and resurface the liquids under there and store these liquids in large devices?

"My engineers tell me that in order to achieve this, we will have to use the compound all the way down to the liquid and beyond, but it can be done."

An adult male at the back of the room rose to speak.

"Do you know of the large hole to the right of the community?"

"I do."

"We tried to dig for liquid many, many generations ago and all we accomplished was to have the top and middle layers cave in as the liquid was removed. How are we going to keep this from happening again?"

"I believe it can be done if we make sure the hole is supported as we dig down. I realize how soft the second layer is, but I truly believe if we use a hard enough compound, we will end up with a way to the liquid and a permanent access to it."

They continued to discuss the possibilities of going after the liquid that had seeped into the planet. Those who had either lost interest or had other pressing things to do left and let Grorth and those who chose to explore the idea of liquid recovery get on with it.

The nua was only in its infancy and already the downpour of liquid was making itself felt. Many had taken note that each nua seemed more severe than the one before and many of these wondered when it would end. There weren't any recordings of nuas and naus worse than the ones they had been experiencing these past few revolutions and some of them were wondering when it would end. Some of the elder members of the community had stories passed down from their ancestors of blistering nau and torrential nua but none alive had seen them. Until now.

It was not long before all of the liquid storage devices were full and the low lying surface was filling with liquid. The Council feared for the community and had people watch the flows closely.

The liquid fell, and kept falling, sun and darkness, for rotations. Even the children started complaining about not being able to get rest for the noise on their abode tops and not being able to go outside without getting thoroughly sopping.

The once dry streambeds had become rivers and the riverbeds small lakes and yet the liquid fell. There were times when one couldn't see across to the next abode for the liquid and somehow it just came down harder. There seemed to be no end to it. It made the last bad one seem like a small cascade. But at least, from the experiences of the last bad nua, everyone had learned how to deal with their abodes, animals and family units.

Then, the nua reached its end and the community felt a great sense of relief. No animals, abode pets or nutritional items had been lost and no children separated from their family units.

Because they had devised a way to keep the saline and fresh liquid separate, they were spared the time of thirst the last nua had brought. They had enough liquid to last and even some left over. Many of the female adults decided to take advantage of this and they planted new growth that needed tending, not just those that had survived in the climate naturally. They also, either by choice or by accident, allowed the liquid bearing plants to become over saturated to grow even bigger, thus giving the community yet another source of liquid in times of need.

It was also because of the abundance of liquid from the nua that the Council put off trying to bring the liquid up from below the surface. They felt since there was not longer the lack they could afford to take more time to plan the process properly. Besides, they had to allow the surface to dry and that alone could take many rotations. There was more liquid lying on the surface than ever before and therefore more soil and liquid mixture to walk through. Never had anyone seen such a mess after a nua. It would take until the next nua to clean the community, even with the heat that was arriving shortly.

Could things get any worse?

The Nau

The time of flowers was more spectacular than ever before and with the fragrances came love. There were enough flowers this nau to fill the requirements of all betrothals, births and other celebrations without even leaving open spots in the fields. People gave flowers, walked through the flowers and lay in the flowers until they were sick of flowers. It was wonderful. Short lived, but wonderful; much shorter, come to think of it, than past revolutions, also, and the heat much more intense than before.

The heat was tremendous very early on and the call for liquid was great but the storage devices were full. No one had any worries about the nau and liquid. They just concerned themselves with staying out of the heat, which seemed almost impossible. Even the coolants they had relied on in past revolutions so successfully could not keep up.

The nau was half way through when some abodes found their supply of liquid going faster than expected. Rationing was started as a 'just to be on the side of safety' thought and some even laughed when told about it. There had never been so much stored liquid before. What was the Council worried about? They were turning into old female adults.

The temperature continued to climb.

The levels of liquid continued to drop.

The huge amounts of coolant slowly disappeared.

Then, as in all other naus, the people adjusted and became able to conduct their lives normally in the heat. Even the smallest of children started to stay out of doors again and turn brown in the sun.

The Council realized, however, they were going to have to go after the subsurface liquid. The Council asked the engineers had estimated it would take several rotations for the preparations alone so they wasted no more time. Morgos wanted to be fully prepared. If they did not need the extra liquid, so be it. But he didn't want to have his people suffer and have the liquid still under the surface.

The digging went on as did life in the community. The first lot of compound was made and the first few meters of hole dug and lined. The heat was at its highest and the ladies found it too hot to tend to their plantings so they allowed the plants to die. Justification for the use of liquid to keep the flowers alive could not be found, especially with the community growing by leaps and bounds, which put an even greater burden on the limited liquid supplies. It also did not take long to use all of the liquid stored in the water-bearing plants that only rotations before had been so big and full.

Then the first death amongst the prisoners was confirmed. Morgos was called to the valley and he was to join up with the medical unit there. Codid accompanied Morgos to the valley because of his relationship to Cau. If Cau was the one who had died, Codid would be allowed to perform the Death of a Relative chant at the bedside of the departed. If it was not Cau, Codid would still be allowed to do the Death chant in honour of his comrade. The punishment said the prisoner could not be buried in the community, but no one would deny him his burial rites. That just wasn't done, no matter what the dead had done in life.

But the death was not Cau's. He met Morgos and Codid at the entrance to the valley and handed Morgos a small mound of precious salt. It was the Rnite condolence ritual expressing their sorrow for the death but wishing those who survived a long life. Morgos accepted the salt.

The guards then took Morgos and Codid across the valley floor. Because transporters were forbidden there because of the possibility of escape, the four of them had to walk. Fortunately it was a short walk and they arrived at Tae's hut in good speed. There they found, lying on his sleeping platform, Tae. Morgos looked down at the remains of the former Ruling Council's Leader, leaned over and after ensuring himself Tae was really gone, he spat in the face of the adult male who had made everyone's life horribly miserable for so long.

"Bury him," he said. "Bury him deep. I want to be able to ensure our people this quisling is really dead." He then turned and left the abode and started walking across the valley floor.

"Do you not want to know what killed him, Morgos?" asked one of the medical unit members.

Morgos' answer was simple, to the point and final.

"No."

There was no mourning the death of Tae, nor was there any burial ritual performed in the community or at the traditional ceremony performed at the next Council gathering; nor was he honoured with a plaque in the Hall of the Dead. His assigned space would remain empty for eternity. Hardly anyone even took notice of the announcement when it was made, which was done only out of respect to those Tae had left behind, who really didn't care one way or another. Those who did notice did so only as a passing glance. Not even his family mourned his passing because his death was not a loss to them. It was only relief. Tae's death meant his family members and former friends could be released from the guilt by association law and get on with their lives. Within seven rotations it was as if Tae had never existed. His family was welcomed back into the society of the community and his friends picked up the threads of their lives to carry on as if he had never entered their thoughts, or lives, in the first place. His name had been stricken from all records of Kladax when he had first been found guilty and it was replaced with the words 'He Who We Do Not Mention Or Remember'. According to law, and emotion, Kladax never had a member of the community called Tae. What a legacy to leave, Grorth thought, but Tae had no one to blame but Tae himself.

The nau came to a close with the digging still being done and the supplies of liquid almost gone. The temperature never dipped below the hottest recorded for each sun and the darkness periods were sweltering. Children and elders alike had trouble sleeping and many families would take strolls in the middle of the darkness in search of cooler areas. None were found, but the time they spent together was time not soon forgotten. It was on such a night that the first rumblings were to be heard. The ones to hear it ran in the direction the noise had come and what they found brought them to a sudden halt. The light of the moons led the way and it was because of the light they were able to stop in time.

The ground had opened up right in front of them and they were looking down into a crevasse as deep as any of them had ever seen. More ground gave way as they stood on the edge and they had to turn and run to keep from being taken down. Their terrified screams brought many of the community racing toward them to see what was happening.

By the time the sun rose the crevasse stretched from the edge of the community to the hills that surrounded the now stranded forbidden valley and as far as the eye could see in either direction, left or right. The abodes that were at the edge of the community were hastily emptied and some none too soon, for they were quickly swallowed by the ever increasing hole which by this time was also quickly filling with liquid from beneath the surface. Morgos had voiced over to the other side of the landmass and had prepared them for the arrival of those that survived. Space was found and when the available areas were full, more were created.

But the hole seemed to be growing faster than the community could go. Some did not make it and they lost not only everything they owned, but some lost loved ones to the panic and the hole. But there wasn't time to grieve. They had to keep moving. They had to find the strength to move even faster than they had been. Still, it wasn't fast enough.

"Morgos?" asked one of the lesser members of the Council. "What can we do about the remaining prisoners? We can't just leave them. What of the guards who remain out there with them? We must try to save them." He knew he was talking nonsense, but he had to get the words out before the burden of guilt sent him mad.

Morgos put his hand on the younger adult male's shoulder and made eye contact. Neither said a word but they understood each other fully. Their world was disappearing and Morgos could not help but wonder what difference one little ship would have made it they had allowed it to continue its orbit far above them. The young adult male broke down and cried. He had accepted the guards and prisoners were no more. Morgos gathered him up into his arms and held him until the sobs subsided. He had done what so many had wanted to do but did not have the time to think about. They were far too busy trying to save themselves to even think of the prisoners or the guards and now it was far too late. When they did, more tears would come and there would be comfort for them, also.

Morgos and the young male adult turned and went back to work. They had spent such a little time, but it was very valuable time and they rushed to make up for it. There were still so many to get to safety and time was running out. The portable transports were constantly being moved back, loaded and moved back again to protect itself from being lost and to send people over. Those that could made their way to the grounded transporters in great numbers. The faster all of them worked, the faster they had to go.

The people on the other side of the landmass greeted the new comers, got their possessions out of the transporters and were ready to greet the next ones arriving. Meanwhile, they had their own preparations for the coming nua to complete. The new arrivals wasted no time in lending hands toward these preparations and the help was more than welcome.

An astute youth of the community had been reading the ancient history books of Kladax and found their land was once lush with large plant life, animals and flowing liquid. He found the pictures so amazing he had trouble believing they had been real. The land he knew was arid, hot and desolate.

He read on and found the ancients had culled the plant life for abodes and had not taken the precaution of ensuring the root systems remained and the few plants that remained withered and died. Some had tried to replant those they had taken but it was too little too late and the newly planted did not develop the root systems needed to reach the subsurface liquid and strength to keep the soil together.

He went on to find the effects of this and climate change explained a great deal of what had happened to the planet, but there were still factors that he had not found when the alarm was sounded. He threw his books aside, where they were to lay untouched from then on, and ran to the transporters. There were so many arriving everyone was being called to help and he wasted no time getting there.

Another member of the community had volunteered to keep the count of the new comers and people were arriving so quickly he had to enlist the aide of another. Then they each enlisted the aide of one more and they were finally able to keep up. There wasn't time upon arrival for proper greetings and everyone understood this. There would be plenty of time for that later. But when the transporters fell silent, less than half of the other community had arrived. Where was Grorth? Naeho? Wahon? Morgos? Enu? Smun? Travor? So many others.

The Ruling Council's Leader from this community met with the representatives on his Council from the other community to query what might have caused the people to stop arriving.

"There are no more," was the only thing the representative could say. "There are no more."

The sadness was felt throughout the community and left no one untouched. Female adults. Male adults. Children. Lost forever. Those who had arrived felt guilt because they had survived and those from the new community felt lose of brothers and sisters they had never met. The Ceremony for the Dead was held the next sun and not a soul stayed in their abodes or went to their workstations.

"They died as they lived," the Ruling Council's Leader said. "They fought hard to live and ensure a future for their children. They did what had to be done to help make this come to be. Now they are with Olag and He is taking them under His wing.

"Those who have joined us," and he panned his arm around the gathered survivors, "have been truly blessed to have made it this far. They entered the transporters with full faith that they would work and get them here. They had full faith that we would embrace them and have space ready for them. Both came to be.

"Now they must have faith that their friends and families are waiting for them with Olag and they will. One rotation, meet again."

There then followed the reading of the list of those families who did not come through the transporter. The list was long and the weeping longer. When it was over, the new comers were led to their new abodes and their new lives.

The Ruling Council's Leader called a gathering for the next sun to discuss the future of the community and the planet itself. It had always been a struggle during the nau but with even more people the struggle would be that much harder. The nutritional requirements alone would put a strain on the community and the growers would have to work over time to ensure enough for all. Would the surface they had suitable for plants survive the extra demand they were going to place on it?

The workers went hard to it building more liquid storage devices and abodes for their new neighbours. There would be plenty of liquid and catching it wouldn't be a problem. The workers went throughout the darkness and changed shifts at the rising sun. The growers hurried to find enough to plant so it would have time to grow before the nua and become too wet.

If anyone had taken the time to ask, those who worked harder would have said it was hard but enjoyable. They were able to help the new comers and they were helping themselves by working side-by-side with their counterparts. Everyone was getting acquainted and new bonds were forming. Life was looking good for one and all. But they had to hurry and there would be time for visiting later.

But before the end of the next darkness, while some took a well deserved rest, a lone male walked screamed as he heard a mighty roar and then fell into a hole that had not been there moments before. The moons were absent this darkness with the stars giving off very little light and since he was away from the community and its lighting he had had only his memory to lead him on his walk.

Scores of members of the community ran to the walker's aide not because of hearing his screams but because of the immense noise the falling surface had made. But they were too late and the sight that was waiting for them was terrifying. They were barely able to catch themselves before the same fate as their friend and neighbour met them. The ground was disappearing! The planet was collapsing! It wasn't an isolated area on the other side of the landmass after all! It had come to them, also! The whole community would disappear just like the other one did and no one could stop it.

The rising sun found this community scrambling to save itself as the other had but this time there was no where to go. The liquid was rising even faster than ever before and the ground was disappearing faster than an adult male could run. No one could make themselves heard above the din and those that may have temporarily been pulled back from the ever enlarging hole went to Olag looking, in some cases, right at another person, screaming, but not heard. Some of the community just stood where they were and allowed themselves to be swallowed up, too frightened to move, while others tried to transport themselves anywhere but where they were. Others fell to their knees, pleading with Olag to save them. There was an adult male on his stomach holding on to the hands of another male adult, trying to keep him from falling. The ground disintegrated beneath him and they both disappeared. Others were running away from the crevasse as quickly as they could only to find it wasn't fast enough. The heating units in the few remaining abodes had set fires that no one could fight and animals were running wild. The noises blended together so one could not be differentiated from another.

The Ruling Council's Leader stood on the raised platform and watched his people disappear while not knowing what to do and pulling at the top of his head with both hands. When he turned to see how far they had run, he saw nothing but emptiness. The crevasse had completely encircled his world and he was left standing alone, his eyes almost coming out of his head with fright and bewilderment. He raised his hands to Olag and began laughing. His laughter turned to a blood-curdling scream that no one else heard and it went on until he himself disappeared.

The two ends of the great sea came together in crashing waves that sent spray one thousand measures into the air. It was a spectacle like no other. But there wasn't anyone left to record the marvel of it all. When the liquid finally settled down into a gentle lapping wave, debris floated for a moment and then it, too, was swallowed up.

The darkness period came.

The Nua

The nua came and fell softly on the sea.

The nau followed with the heat drying up very little of the liquid that had become Kladax. The heat warmed the liquid during the sun and the coolness of the darkness chilled it.

This cycle went on for many millennia, until the ooze at the bottom spit forth its secrets. At that time, the smallest of small found its way to the surface where it joined with another of its kind and they became three. Not far away two others split in two and became four. A few measurements away from them a single cell divided many times to create the smallest of creatures. It was the beginning of new life on Kladax.

Maybe this time it would last.

Maybe this time there would be no higher life forms than these.

Maybe this time the simple organisms would become the mighty.

Then there would be no fighting, no taking of minerals, no hunting for liquid beyond what they already had.

Maybe this time it would be great.

Maybe.